A.J. Vaughan

Personal Record of the Thirteenth Regiment, Tennessee Infantry

Outlook

A.J. Vaughan

Personal Record of the Thirteenth Regiment, Tennessee Infantry

1. Auflage | ISBN: 978-3-73262-332-7

Erscheinungsort: Frankfurt am Main, Deutschland

Erscheinungsjahr: 2018

Outlook Verlag GmbH, Frankfurt.

A.J. Vaughan

Personal Record of the Thirteenth Regiment, Tennessee Infantry

Outlook

A. J. VAUGHAN

PERSONAL RECORD OF THE THIRTEENTH REGIMENT, TENNESSEE INFANTRY.

BY ITS OLD COMMANDER.

Price, 75 cents.

PRESS OF S. C. TOOF & CO.
MEMPHIS.
1897.

MOST AFFECTIONATELY DEDICATED
TO THE
NOBLE MOTHERS AND WIVES
OF THE
TRUE AND HEROIC MEN WHO FOR FOUR YEARS
FOLLOWED THE CONFEDERATE FLAG,
AND WHO WERE WILLING TO LAY DOWN THEIR
LIVES IN DEFENSE OF THAT CAUSE THEY
BELIEVED RIGHT AND JUST.

A. J. VAUGHAN.

PREFACE.

MY OLD COMRADES:

In writing out this record I have gone back to the morning time of my own life, and lived once more in that other day that not only tried, but proved men's souls. Insignificant as my work may appear as a literary production, it carries with it the most sacred memories of the past. In writing, I have lived over again the days when the boom of cannon, the rattle of musketry and the old rebel yell were familiar sounds to our ears. If a shade of mournfulness hovers over the failure of the cause for which these brave men fought and many fell, it is not a mournfulness born of regret. When we who wore the gray put away forever the musket and sword—and let me say, my comrades, swords and muskets that had been bravely borne—we did so in sorrow but not in malice or hate. And today, I am sure, where one of the old regiment lingers yet a little while this side of the dark river, he accepts in good faith the terms of his parole, and is a peaceful and faithful citizen of the United States; not only faithful, but as loyal to the stars and stripes as we were once to that other flag which we followed for four long years, and which was woven from an honest belief of a people's need.

Now, to my old comrades, whether in flesh or spirit, to whom this little compilation has carried me back with such tremendous force, and to keep alive whose fair fame I have written, I can only say as my last words—God bless you!

A. J. VAUGHAN.

The Thirteenth Regiment,

TENNESSEE INFANTRY.

This was one of the regiments that made Cheatham's Division, and Smith's-Vaughan's and Gordon's Brigades so famous in the Army of Tennessee. It was organized and mustered into service on the third day of June, 1861, in answer to a call of Governor Isham G. Harris for seventy-five thousand volunteers. At that time it was the seventh infantry regiment organized in West Tennessee and the thirteenth in the State. It was made up of the "flower of the South" young men, most of whom were fresh from the best institutions of learning—aspiring, hopeful and ambitious—sons of men of education, wealth and influence—the very best material for volunteer service. It was composed of ten full companies—five from Fayette county, one from Shelby, one from Dyer, one from McNairy, one from Gibson, and one from Henderson, and were as follow:

Company A, Fayette Rifles, Captain William Burton of Somerville, Tenn.

Company B, Macon Grays, Captain J. L. Granberry, Macon, Tenn.

Company C, Secession Guards, organized at Germantown, Tenn., and composed of Mississippians and Tennesseeans, Captain John H. Morgan, Horn Lake, Miss.

Company D, Yorkville Rifles, Captain John Wilkins, Yorkville, Tenn.

Company E, Dixie Rifles, organized at Moscow, Tenn., and composed of Tennesseeans and Mississippians, Captain A. J. Vaughan, Marshall county, Miss.

Company F, Wright Boys, Captain Jno. V. Wright, Purdy, McNairy county, Tenn.

Company G, Gaines Invincibles, Captain W. E. Winfield, LaGrange, Tenn.

Company H, Yancey Rifles, Captain Robert W. Pittman, Hickory Withe, Tenn.

Company I, Forked Deer Volunteers, Captain G. S. Ross, Forked Deer, Tenn.

Company K, Dyer Grays, Captain S. R. Latta, Dyersburg, Tenn.

On the following day, the 4th of June, the election of field officers was held, and resulted in the election of Captain Jno. V. Wright of Company F as Colonel, Captain A. J. Vaughan of Company E as Lieutenant-Colonel, and Captain W. E. Winfield of Company G as Major.

The regiment was ordered at once by way of Memphis to Randolph, on the Mississippi river, when the organization was completed by the appointment of Lieutenant W. E. Morgan, Company C, Adjutant; Dr. J. A. Forbes, Company E, Surgeon; Dr. B. F. Dickerson, Company I, Assistant Surgeon; W. E. Dyer, Company G, Commissary; L. B. Cabler, Company A, Regimental Quartermaster; Peter Cole, Company H, Sergeant-Major; and W. D. F. Hafford, Chaplain.

The regiment remained at Randolph engaged in drilling, camp duty, etc., until July 26th, when it was ordered to New Madrid, Mo., and placed in a brigade under command of Colonel J. P. McCown, who, under orders from General Gid. J. Pillow, was about to make a campaign into South-west Missouri to prevent reinforcements being sent to the Federal General Lyons, then operating in that section.

On the 18th of August, 1861, the troops were moved in the direction of Benton, Mo., where the Thirteenth Regiment arrived on the 19th. This was the first campaign or march of the regiment, and though in the middle of summer during a severe drouth, under a burning sun and over roads shoe deep in sand and dust, it was cheerfully performed, and showed an endurance and fortitude rarely witnessed in new troops. The object of the campaign being accomplished, the command returned to New Madrid on Sept. 2, and on the following day the regiment was ordered to Hickman, Ky., where it was placed in Cheatham's Brigade. At Hickman, on Sept. 4, 1861, the regiment for the first time caught a glimpse of the "boys in blue" and saw the first "burning of gunpowder," which was an artillery duel between the Federal gunboats and the Confederate land batteries; but it was at long range, no damage was done, and the gunboats were soon withdrawn up the river.

About this time General Leonidas Polk, commanding the Mississippi Department, determined to occupy Columbus, Ky., and ordered General B. F. Cheatham to proceed at once to that point, where the Thirteenth Regiment arrived Sept. 6, 1861, and was among the first, if not the first, to occupy that important position. Nothing but camp duty, throwing up heavy fortifications and hard and constant drilling occurred in the regiment until Nov. 7, when it was reported that the enemy in heavy force was advancing on Columbus on both sides of the river. The long roll was sounded and every regiment reported at once and fell into line on its parade ground. All were excited and anxious to meet the enemy. Soon it was ascertained that a heavy force had disembarked from their gunboats above and were moving down to a point near Belmont, on the opposite side of the river.

The Thirteenth Regiment, under command of Colonel John V. Wright, having been supplied with ammunition, was ordered at once to cross the river and take position on the extreme left of our line of battle near Watson's Battery. Never was a regiment more anxious or more willing to face an enemy. It was the maiden fight of the regiment and every man felt that he was "on his mettle." Though our position was an unfortunate one—in an open field, the enemy being under cover of thick woods—this regiment met the advance with the steadiness of veterans and held its position and fought while comrades fell on every side until the last round of ammunition was exhausted, and the order given to fall back to the river. By the time the regiment reached the river reinforcements had crossed from Columbus which engaged the enemy and checked his further advance. The Thirteenth, obtaining a fresh supply of ammunition, rallied and again advanced gallantly to the contest, which had become fierce and obstinate. In a short time the Federals were driven from their position and fled to their gunboats, hotly pursued by the Confederates. At their gunboats, such was their haste, confusion and disorder that they did not attempt to return the fire. The Federal loss here, as in previous engagements, was heavy.

The loss of the Thirteenth Regiment was heavy; out of one hundred and fourteen killed and wounded, thirty-four were killed on the field, among them the very best men of Tennessee. Their names should never be forgotten, and are as follow:

Company A—A. Middlemus, First Sergeant; A. J. McCully; Mike McCully; Matthew Rhea, First Lieutenant commanding.

Company B—F. M. Stockinger; W. H. Burnett, Second Corporal.

Company C—Arthur R. Pittman; J. W. Rogers; Robt. F. Dukes, Lieutenant; J. P. Farrow; J. W. Harris.

Company D—W. H. Parks; W. H. Polk; Jno. H. Shaw; Albert G. Zaracer; B. M. Dozier.

Company E—S. J. Roberson; Geo. R. Tiller; E. Wales Newby.

Company F—H. H. Barnett; E. H. Hill; John A. Jones, Sr.; C. H. Middleton.

Company G—P. N. D. Bennett; Jno. Mayo; Jno. C. Penn.

Company H—George Hall; Wm. J. Dunlap.

Company I—C. C. Cawhon; L. F. Hamlet; John G. Nesbit; H. H.

Waggoner; James Hamlet.

Company K—Y. W. Hall; K. A. Parrish; Jas. L. Smith.

J. P. Farrow and Wm. J. Dunlap were the first men in the regiment who yielded their young lives in battle to the Confederate cause, and were killed by the first volley of the enemy's fire.

Early in action Colonel John V. Wright was painfully injured in the knee by the fall of his horse which was shot under him. I, who then took command of the regiment, had two horses shot under me: the first at the very commencement of the engagement; the second (which had been cut out of Watson's Battery after its men had been driven from their guns) was shot just as I reached the river bank.

Never did men display more heroic courage and deport themselves in a more soldierlike manner, and while it is impossible in this brief sketch to refer to all the acts of devotion and fidelity to the Southern cause performed by the officers and men of this regiment, Lieutenant Matthew Rhea certainly deserves special mention. As soon as the regiment took position in line of battle, in command of his company (A) he was sent to the extreme left of our line with instruction to extend his line to the river, which he did. By some means the enemy got in between him and the regiment, thus cutting him off. Though surrounded he continued to fight, and rather than surrender his sword, which had been worthily worn by his grandfather, he fell at the hands of the enemy. A braver, truer or more faithful officer never fought for any cause.

About this time, if not on the very day of the battle of Belmont, Colonel John V. Wright was elected to the Confederate Congress, and resigned his position as Colonel of the regiment. No man ever stood higher in the estimation of his soldiers or was more beloved by them.

Upon the resignation of Colonel Wright I was unanimously elected Colonel of the regiment. I was a disciplinarian while on duty of the strictest school, which for the first months of the war made me very unpopular with volunteer soldiers, but only one fight was necessary to satisfy them that an undisciplined army was nothing more than an armed mob. Adjutant W. E. Morgan was now elected Lieutenant-Colonel, and Lieutenant Richard M. Harwell of Company E was appointed Adjutant.

After the battle of Belmont and while at Columbus, Ky., the measles broke out in the regiment, and it was a matter of surprise that there should be so many grown men who had never had the measles. So many were down at one time that there were scarcely enough well ones to wait on the sick, and many died.

Early in the spring it became necessary to move our lines further south, and Columbus was evacuated March 12, 1862. The Thirteenth was ordered to Union City, and four days later to Corinth, Miss., where it arrived March 19, 1862. Before leaving Columbus, however, there had been some changes made in the command. General B. F. Cheatham had been promoted to a division commander, and the Thirteenth was assigned to Colonel R. M. Russell's Brigade, General Chas. Clark's Division. In this brigade and division the regiment remained until after the battle of Shiloh.

About this time the enemy was known to be landing and concentrating a large force at Pittsburg Landing, on the Tennessee river. It was determined by Gen. Albert Sidney Johnston, who had been placed in command, to give battle; so on the 3rd of April, 1862, the regiment, with the whole army, was moved toward the point of attack, but heavy rains and bad roads prevented forming line of battle until the evening of the 5th of April. That night a council of war was held, and though some officers were opposed, an attack was determined upon.

On the morning of the 6th, just as the sun in all its splendor was rising above the horizon, and while in the second line of battle, General Clark rode up to us and stated that Marks' Louisiana Regiment had been repulsed, and asked, "Can you take that battery yonder, which is annoying our troops so much?" Having such unlimited confidence in the Thirteenth, I replied, "We can take it." Whereupon the regiment was moved by the right flank, under cover of a hill, until in proper position, and then fronted the battery and advanced rapidly up the hill. All was well until the crest of the hill was reached, when the enemy opened fire with canister, grape and musketry, which was so severe that it literally tore the regiment in two. But, though, for a moment checked, nothing daunted, our officers and men gallantly stood their ground, and poured into the ranks of the enemy such deadly volleys as to cause them to waver, and then with the "rebel yell" rushed so impetuously upon them that they could no longer stand, precipitately fleeing and leaving battery and dead and wounded on the field.

This was indeed a brilliant charge, and only equaled on that battlefield by the charge made shortly afterward by that magnificent regiment, the Fourth Tennessee. But the loss to the regiment was terrible; some of Tennessee's best blood was shed here, and many a noble spirit sank to rise no more.

The balance of the day the regiment, though not actively engaged, was for the most time under heavy fire in changing and shifting positions and in supporting and relieving other troops. It was present and assisted in capturing Gen. Lew Wallace[1] and his brigade late in the evening on the bank of the Tennessee river, to which point we had driven the enemy. Here, because of the steep bluff, the gunboats could not reach us, and a rain of iron and lead passed over our heads until late in the night. Under orders the regiment retired from the river bank and bivouaced for the night in the enemy's camp, rich with quartermaster's stores, commissary supplies and sutlers' goods.

[1] By oversight I have printed on page 16 the name Lew Wallace. Of course it should have been Gen. Prentice.

Every officer and soldier of the regiment sank to sleep serenaded by the guns from the river, and supposed that the battle was won and the victory ours. But how sadly disappointed next morning, when it was known that Buell had arrived and crossed the river that night with his whole army, and was drawn up in line with fresh troops to renew the contest. Though not anticipating such a state of affairs, the regiment was formed by early dawn and moved forward to meet the enemy as proudly and defiantly as on the day before. But their batteries, within easy range and supported by columns of infantry, opened such a terrible fire of grape and canister that we were forced to retire and seek shelter beyond the next ridge. By this time the whole Confederate forces were hotly engaged, and from right to left was one continuous roar of artillery and musketry. The struggle was terrific, and closer and harder fighting was never done on any battlefield; and though the enemy were held at bay from early dawn till nearly noon, it was apparent that the unequal contest could not be much longer maintained. So the Confederate forces were gradually withdrawn, and the army returned to its old camp grounds at Corinth, Miss. No attempt was made by the enemy to follow. The first day's fight of this battle was the grandest of the war—less friction, more concert of action, more thorough co-operation and better generalship displayed—everything moved with clock-like precision—a master mind directed the whole until General A.
S. Johnston fell.

Throughout the two days' fight every officer and man of the Thirteenth did his whole duty, as shown by the heavy loss in killed and wounded. We lost one hundred and twelve men killed and wounded, and of this number forty- two fell dead on the bloody field, thus sealing their devotion with their lives to the cause they believed right. Their names deserve to be remembered by their countrymen, and are as follow:

Robert Thompson, B. F. Eaton, H. B. Hunt, R. Harrison, J. M. Moore, James Moore, N. Matthews, R. M. Thompson and Lieut. C. H. Whitmore of Company A; J. G. Babbett, Lieut. S. B. Dugan and Henry Walker of Company B; W. B. Dukes, C. P. Graham, H. J. Hutchinson, Thos. Rainey (color bearer) and W. L. Stokes of Company C; Second Lieut. W. F. Cowan, First Lieut. J. W. Cunningham, R. D. Eaton and Capt. John A. Wilkins of Company D; D. C. Arnett, D. C. Bull, J. C. Black and M. C. Grisson of Company E; M. Donelly, J. N. Guthrie, Jno. Morgan, William Saunders, J. D.

Springer and B. Thomas of Company F; M. M. McKinstry, J. H. Brown and J. O. Winfield of Company G; E. O. Chambers, S. O. Cole, D. R. Royster and Carr Young of Company H; Jno. Mitchell, Lewis Roberson, J. N. Vandyke and G. W. Borger of Company I; Carroll Chitwood of Company K.

From the opening to the close of this engagement I was most ably and efficiently assisted in the management and direction of the regiment by Lieut.-Col. W. E. Morgan, Adjutant R. M. Harwell, and Major W. E. Winfield. Adjutant Harwell was painfully wounded in the first engagement but remained at his post of duty until the close of the struggle. Lieut.-Colonel Morgan and Major Winfield had their horses shot, and I had two horses shot under me and was struck by a spent ball that did no serious harm.

While at Corinth, the period for which the regiment had enlisted having expired, it re-enlisted for the war and reorganized. Company A, from some disaffection or dissatisfaction, refused to reorganize, and was consolidated with Company D, and the deficiency supplied by the admission of Company L, Zollicoffer's Avengers, Captain C. B. Jones, of LaGrange, Tenn. On the 28th of April, 1862, the reorganization was perfected by the election of the following officers: I was unanimously re-elected Colonel; W. E. Morgan unanimously re-elected Lieutenant-Colonel; Sergeant-Major P. H. Cole elected Major; Lieut. R. M. Harwell re-elected Adjutant. Many changes were made in line officers, but the writer has no data from which to supply them. While at Corinth the regiment, from the use of bad and unhealthy water, suffered very much with sickness, and many were furloughed on sick leave to recuperate for the summer campaign.

The enemy in the meantime having recovered from the severe blow received at Shiloh commenced to advance on Corinth by gradual approaches, and by the latter part of May was in the vicinity of that place. The regiment was daily engaged in heavy skirmishes, and sometimes in sharp engagements but with small losses. On May 13, 1862, Corinth was evacuated, and the Thirteenth fell back by way of Baldwin to Tupelo, Miss. Here, with good water, the health of the regiment improved rapidly, and with strict discipline and constant drilling we soon became one of the crack regiments in that army.

About this time General Charles Clark, commanding the division, was assigned to another department, and his division broken up and assigned to other commands. The Thirteenth was assigned to Cheatham's Division and General Preston Smith's Brigade, which, on July 10, 1862, was ordered to report to General E. Kirby Smith at Knoxville, Tenn., who was about to make a campaign into Kentucky. Everything being ready the Thirteenth, with the forces under General Smith, moved on the 13th day of August into Kentucky by way of Wilson Gap, and on the 18th of August arrived at Cumberland Gap after a weary and toilsome march of five days. From this point by way of Manchester the forces were moved in the direction of Richmond, Ky. The enemy was watching the movement, and had sent forward General Bull Nelson with a large force of infantry, artillery and cavalry to check our advance. A battle was now imminent.

Early on the morning of August 30 the army was put in motion, and by 8 o'clock while marching up the road a shell from the enemy's battery not far off came whizzing over the head of our advancing column and exploded high in the air. The Thirteenth with the other regiments of the brigade immediately deployed in line of battle on the right of the road, when Allen's sharpshooters under command of Lieut. Creighton were sent forward and deployed as skirmishers, with instructions to feel the enemy and develop their position. This being done the regiment with the brigade was ordered to advance, and in a short time a most terrific fire was opened by both sides from one end of the line to the other. The enemy occupied a strong position and stubbornly held their ground, but onward the Confederates continued to march, when, with a charge and a yell in front and a volley on their flank, which General Smith with the One Hundred and Fifty-fourth Sr. had succeeded in reaching, the enemy precipitately fled, hotly pursued and pressed by the Confederates. The enemy lay thick upon the field, and their loss was heavy. The Thirteenth's loss was also heavy in officers and men, and among them some of Tennessee's best and bravest soldiers.

It was in this first engagement that Lieutenant Edward Lanier of Company G was killed, a young, brilliant and gallant officer who, had he lived, would either as citizen or soldier have inscribed his name high up on the roll of fame. Gifted by nature, young, aspiring and ambitious it seemed hard that he should have been stricken down at the very threshold of his manhood. A truer soldier never shed his blood on his country's altar. Here, too, General Pat Cleburne was wounded in the mouth, and had to retire from the field, whereupon the command of the division devolved upon Brigadier-General Preston Smith, and that of the brigade on me, and that of the regiment on Lieutenant-Colonel W. E. Morgan.

The enemy after retiring a couple of miles made a second stand, but so impetuous was the second attack that after a short engagement they broke in disorder and confusion, and did not halt until at or near Richmond, where for the last time they made a stand, and it was here that they were completely routed and demoralized.

This was the most complete victory gained during the war in which the Thirteenth participated. Nothing escaped. All the enemy's artillery, their artillery horses, their transportation, quartermaster and commissary supplies, together with all their camp equipage fell into the hands of the Confederates. In this engagement our forces captured and paroled more officers and men than General E. Kirby Smith had in his command. The Thirteenth did its whole duty, as attested by the killed on that battlefield as follow: R. A. Donalson, W. L. Fullerton, S. G. Lawrence, Company A; T. F. Gaither, Company B; W. L. Rhodes, Company C; Jas. J. Lawrence, W. H. Minter, Company D; T. M. Ballard, Company E; H. L. Winningham, Company F; Lieutenant Edward Lanier, Edward Dicks, Company G; Wm. Claiburn, R. H. Crouch, Company H; John Reed, R. R. Stone, B. F. Holtom, Company I; John H. Gates, B. G. Sims, H. A. Gray, J. S. Jenkins, M. R. Winfield, B. W. Wilkerson, Company L.

In this battle I received from the hands of a captain of an Indiana company a beautiful and highly ornamented sword, which had been presented to him by the citizens of his town when he started to the war. After the first attack the Federal captain was retreating with his company when he was shot in the leg. Unable to proceed further a private of the Thirteenth ran up to him and ordered the surrender of his sword. This he refused to do, saying that he would surrender it to an officer, but never to a private. This so enraged the private that he was in the very act of shooting him when I rode up and ordered him not to shoot a prisoner, whereupon the officer extended to me his sword, and thanked me for saving his life. I wore this sword a long time, but while on leave of absence left it in charge of a young Confederate officer who, being insulted by a negro, broke it over his head.

After the battle of Richmond the Thirteenth with the brigade marched to Lexington, Ky.; thence to Cynthiana, thence to Covington, thence to Frankfort, and joined Gen. Bragg's army just before the battle of Perryville, where it rejoined Cheatham's Division.

The next engagement was the battle of Perryville, which was fought on October 8, 1862. In this battle the Thirteenth with the brigade was not actively engaged, but was held in reserve, and with the brigade acted as rear guard to the army on its march out of Kentucky.

Our march into Kentucky was an ovation. We were the first infantry troops to enter that part of the State, and as soon as we crossed the mountains and struck the Blue Grass region, the demonstration of sympathy for the South and the hearty welcome extended us filled every heart with profound gratitude. Citizens all along our line of march received us with open arms, and showed us every hospitality. When we halted for the night, droves of fattest cattle, herds of the fattest sheep, and wagonloads of corn and hay, were driven to our camp. Even the women—God bless them—brought to our soldiers the delicacies of the table and garden. We thought that Kentucky was ours, and that no Federal force would invade her beautiful territory; but, alas! how soon the scene shifted.

The retreat out of Kentucky was one of greater trial and hardship than any march made during the war. Over a rough and barren country, without shoes and thinly clad, with scarcely anything to eat, the suffering was great, yet it was borne with fortitude and without a murmur.

The regiment, with the army, reached Knoxville on October 24, 1862. From Knoxville the Thirteenth was moved by rail to Tullahoma, where it received a fresh supply of clothing, blankets, shoes, etc., which was so much needed. After a few weeks' rest we were marched to Murfreesboro, where we arrived the latter part of November, 1862. It was here that smallpox broke out in the regiment, and it was detached from the brigade, but by strict quarantine and vaccination it was soon checked—not, however, without the loss of some good soldiers.

Early on the morning of December 30, 1862, we commenced that hard-fought and stubbornly-contested battle of Murfreesboro, or Stone River. It was a most terrific contest—one that brought forth those shining and brilliant qualities of the Southern volunteer which made him so renowned in the Mexican and other wars. In the absence of Brigadier-General Preston Smith, I was in command of the brigade and Lieutenant-Col. W. E. Morgan in command of the regiment. In this fight the Thirteenth, as in every other from Belmont to Murfreesboro, took an active part, and did its whole duty and gathered fresh laurels. It was the most satisfactory fight, both to the officers and men, that was made by the regiment during the war. With the exception of a slight check in the morning, it drove the enemy from every position from early dawn till late in the evening; and though every inch of ground was fiercely contested, the regiment never faltered, but onward like an avalanche it swept everything before it. I had two horses shot under me, and the horse of every field and staff officer of the regiment was killed.

In this engagement I witnessed an exhibition of discipline and coolness that I never saw on any other battlefield. We had in our front and opposed to us a brigade of United States Regulars; they were formed in two lines of battle some distance apart. Firing as we advanced, their first line waited until we got within easy range and then coolly delivered their fire; without waiting to reload they faced to the rear and double-quicked through their second line and reformed in line of battle. The second line then awaited our approach, and though their men were falling fast around them, they coolly delivered their fire and retired through the first line and reformed in line of battle; and thus they continued to fire and fall back until they were driven across a large field. Their lines were plainly marked by their dead, who lay thick upon the ground.

These were Americans fighting Americans—the one, the trained soldier, who fought because he was ordered to do so, and because of the old flag and that Union which he believed ought to be eternal; the other, the Southern volunteer, who fought because he believed that his home and fireside were invaded and that his constitutional rights were trampled upon. Both exhibited a courage which commands the world's admiration.

In this battle a battery of four beautiful Napoleon guns was captured from the Federals. Four divisions of our army claimed to have participated in the capture, and each division laid claims to the battery. A conference of the officers of the divisions was called, and after a full discussion and careful consideration of the claims of each division, it was decided that one of the guns should be given to each division, and that upon it should be inscribed the name of the most gallant and meritorious soldier who fell on that battlefield. One of the guns was given to Cheatham's Division and assigned to Preston Smith's Brigade. At that time I was Colonel of the Thirteenth Tennessee Regiment and W. E. Morgan Lieutenant-Colonel; but in the absence of Gen. Preston Smith I commanded the brigade and Lieutenant-Colonel Morgan the regiment. He fell in the first day's fight, and by unanimous consent his name was inscribed upon the gun, and read as follows: "Lieutenant-Colonel W. E. Morgan, Thirteenth Tennessee Regiment, Pres. Smith's Brigade, Cheatham's Division, Polk's Corps." This gun was assigned to Scott's Battery, and at the battle of Chickamauga it was skillfully handled and did effective work in checking the advance of the Federals; but when Gen. Grant attacked our lines at Missionary Ridge, it was recaptured by the Federal forces, and today it stands a silent sentinel in the beautiful "Park of Gettysburg." Captured and recaptured on two famous battlefields, it stands there a proof of the heroism of both sides; it stands there as ready to do service for the stars and stripes as it once did for that other flag which lived its brief life always in the storm of battle, and which, without dishonor, was laid aside and folded forever, with no other stain upon its fold than that of heroes' blood shed to give it life.

Here it was that Lieutenant-Colonel W. E. Morgan, the pride of the regiment and the hero of so many brilliant achievements, fell mortally wounded; he fought his way up from Lieutenant of his company (C) to Lieutenant-Colonel of the regiment, and no promotion was ever more deserved. Major P. H. Cole also fell in this battle; he, too, deserves the gratitude of his countrymen for the faithful discharge of his duty. It was here, too, that Private W. A. Abernathy was killed; though a mere youth he was endowed with all of those sterling qualities which make heroes; he was every inch a soldier; whether on the march, in the camp, or on the field of battle, he was the life and pride of his comrades; though offered promotion he always refused, saying he preferred fighting in the ranks. Here, too, J. A. Stone, though severely wounded, bound up his wounds and returned to his company, remaining with it and leading every charge during the day.

Upon the fall of Lieutenant-Colonel W. E. Morgan and Major P. H. Cole, R. F. Lanier, senior Captain, the bravest of the brave, took command of the regiment and led it throughout the remainder of the fight with skill and judgment, and made for himself a character for dash and daring that followed him throughout the war; no man in the army of Tennessee was more devoted to the Southern cause.

The regiment went into this battle with two hundred and twenty-six officers and men, and lost in killed and wounded one hundred and ten. Twenty-eight were killed and their names should be ever remembered with affection. They are:

J. C. Kelly, Company A; G. H. Adams, Logan McKinstry, W. B. Reed, W. R. Carter, J. C. Tharp, E. M. Waller, Company B; Boggan Cash, Wayne Holman, Lieutenant-Colonel W. E. Morgan, Captain John H. Morgan, Palmer P. Tuggle, Company C; W. A. Abernathy, William Greene, Company E; M. N. Burns, Company F; J. W. Jones, Otey Gloster, W. H. Simmons, Company G; Maj. P. H. Cole, T. J. Forgey, S. D. Aikin, Company H; J. McLaughlin, D. R. Tillman, J. H. McLaughlin, Company I; James F. Dukes, Carter E. Skipwith, Company K; R. J. Bailey, Company L. Boggan Cash was the only one whose fate was not absolutely known. He was in every charge of his company and could not have been wounded or captured, as none of the ground fought over was reoccupied by the enemy. He was a brave and true soldier and always at his post of duty.

On the night of the first day's fight General Preston Smith returned to the brigade and assumed command, and I returned to the regiment. In the second day's fight the regiment was not actively engaged and lost no men. On the night of January 2, 1863, the regiment with the brigade was withdrawn toward Murfreesboro, and the retreat to Shelbyville commenced, which point the regiment reached the next day and went into camp. The enemy did not attempt to follow.

At Shelbyville the Thirteenth and One Hundred and Fifty-fourth Sr. Regiments, having become so reduced in numbers, were consolidated. I was retained as Colonel. Captain R. W. Pittman of the Thirteenth, who had been promoted to Lieutenant-Colonel, was retained with same rank, and Major John W. Dawson of the One Hundred and Fifty-fourth Sr. as Major. Though consolidated, neither regiment ever lost its identity, and each was known to the close of the war by its original regimental appellation. From Belmont to Murfreesboro they had fought side by side on every battlefield. In daylight or in darkness, in victory or in defeat, they had stood shoulder to shoulder. Each knew the worth and value of the other and both had but one purpose in view —and that purpose, even to the extent of their lives, was to maintain the honor of Tennessee and uphold the Confederacy. From this time to the close of the war the history of the two regiments was one common history. The glory of the one was the pride of the other, and neither ever lost hope until the Confederate banner went down forever.

From Shelbyville the army fell back across the Cumberland mountains, thus occupying the same position it did twelve months previous, and before it started into Kentucky. Tennesseeans for the second time saw their section abandoned, yet true to the Southern cause, cheerfully followed the fortunes of the Confederate flag.

The next important event in the history of the regiment was the hard-fought battle of Chickamauga, on September 19 and 20, 1863. It was the first battle after the two regiments had been consolidated that they had fought, and each sustained its former record and gathered fresh laurels. After two days of grand and magnificent fighting the enemy was completely routed and victory perched on the Confederate banner; but, alas! its fruits were lost by the tardy movements of the army in following up the victory. It is not for the writer to say who was at fault, but it was apparent to all that some one was to blame.

The loss in killed and wounded on both sides was exceedingly heavy, and the Thirteenth lost some of its best officers and bravest men. It was here, on the night of the first day's fight (Sept. 19, 1863), that General Preston Smith fell. The circumstances of his death are worthy of record here.

After heavy fighting all day, Cheatham's Division was formed in the second line of battle, and Preston Smith's Brigade was ordered to keep within five hundred paces of Deshler's Texas Brigade of the first line. The two lines were ordered forward with instructions to march directly to the front; but Deshler's Brigade, on account of obstructions and the irregularity of the ground, instead of marching directly to the front, obliqued to the left and passed unnoticed an isolated regiment which proved to be the Seventy-seventh Pennsylvania, which had in some unaccountable manner become separated from the Federal army. Smith's Brigade, marching directly to the front, was approaching too near the first line, when Gen. Smith, thinking it was getting too close, as he supposed, to Deshler's Brigade, ordered a halt and rode forward with his volunteer aid, Captain King of Georgia, to see why, as he thought, Deshler's Brigade had halted. Riding up to the Federal regiment he was discovered to be a Confederate officer and was fired upon and instantly killed, as was Captain King. It was now becoming dark, and I being on the right, and also supposing that Deshler's Brigade had halted, I rode forward with Captain John Donaldson at my side to inquire the cause. When within thirty or forty yards of the regiment a Federal soldier jumped up from under a bush, advanced to me, supposing me to be a Federal officer, and inquired, "Where is the enemy?" Discovering his mistake, he jerked up his gun and without taking aim, fired. The load passed just in front of my breast into the body of Captain Donaldson, who fell a corpse. I ordered the Federal to be fired upon, which was done by the Twelfth Tennessee. In shooting at the Federal soldier their balls ranged into the ranks of the Federal regiment, when they called out, "Don't shoot! don't shoot! we surrender!" Whereupon I rode forward and ordered the regiment to ground arms and surrender their flag, which I received from the color-bearer, and turned over the regiment of prisoners to Captain Carthall of the Twelfth, who marched them to the rear. Thus fell General Preston Smith and his faithful aid Captain King, and Inspector- General Donaldson. I now took command of the Brigade and a short time after was promoted to Brigadier-General.

After the battle of Chickamauga, Cheatham's Division was the first to move and to advance toward Chattanooga, to which point the enemy had retreated, and the Thirteenth was among the first to drive in the enemy's pickets from Missionary Ridge. In doing so, however, Company C of the regiment lost one of her truest and most faithful officers, Lieutenant Henry Brooks, who fell at the head of his command in the full discharge of his duty, admired and loved by his comrades and superior officers.

The next move of the regiment was in the direction of Knoxville to reinforce General Longstreet, but on arriving at Sweetwater news was received of his repulse, and the regiment returned to the old division on Missionary Ridge.

It was now known that the Federals were strongly fortified in Chattanooga, had been heavily reinforced, and were preparing for an advance on the Confederates occupying Missionary Ridge and Lookout Mountain. On November 25, about noon, the Federals advanced in overwhelming numbers, and like an avalanche swept the Confederate lines from Missionary Ridge, though the One Hundred and Fifty-fourth and Thirteenth kept the Federals back in their front until flanked on their left. At this time these two regiments did some of the grandest and most heroic fighting they had done during the war, and though forced to fall back, they contested every inch of ground with that heroism which had characterized them on every battlefield. Night coming on, the Confederates crossed Chickamauga Creek and retired to Dalton, Ga., where our army went into winter quarters.

At Dalton General Braxton Bragg was relieved of command and General Joseph E. Johnston appointed to the command of the army. His appointment was joyfully received by the whole army. Its morale commenced at once to improve, and by early spring it was in splendid fighting condition.

Early in May, 1864, the enemy 100,000 strong made an advance, and it was supposed from the overwhelming numbers of Sherman's army that he would give battle in front of Dalton, but after trying two or more days to dislodge the Confederates, he commenced his flank movement under cover of Rocky Face Ridge. This forced the withdrawal of the Confederates from Dalton to Resaca. The Thirteenth and One Hundred and Fifty-fourth were the first to arrive at Resaca, where they found General Canty's Division skirmishing with the enemy. The enemy was held in check until sufficient reinforcements arrived to drive Sherman back through Black Snake Gap. It was here that the writer, standing by the side of General Johnston (who was intently watching the skirmish line), heard him say that never in his life had he seen skirmishers behave better, or handled with more skill, and turning to the writer, asked: "Do you know to what command they belong and who is their commander?" The writer replied that they were commanded by Lieutenant-Colonel John W. Dawson and belonged to the Thirteenth and One Hundred and Fifty-fourth Tennessee Regiments, Vaughan's Brigade, Cheatham's Division.

From Resaca the regiment fell back to Adairsville, where it had a sharp engagement and inflicted a heavy loss upon the enemy. Thence to Cassville, where everything indicated a pitched battle, and never was the regiment, in fact, the whole army, in better condition. Its morale had improved every day since Johnston assumed command, and it was confidently believed by both officers and men that whenever battle was given, victory was certain. But from some cause battle was not given. It was here that the Thirteenth and One Hundred and Fifty-fourth Regiments had the highest compliment paid them during the war. After the line of battle was formed and every brigade and division in position, General Cheatham was ordered by General Johnston to furnish the best regiment in his division to bring on the engagement. The Thirteenth and One Hundred and Fifty-fourth were furnished.

The next hard fighting done by the regiment was at New Hope Church and Lost Mountain, then on the Kennesaw line at what was known as "dead angle." It was here that Hooker, with that splendid fighting corps of his, made the attack and was so signally repulsed. In column seven lines deep, with not a cap on the guns of the first two lines, he attempted to storm our position. Never did men march into the very jaws of death with a firmer tread and with more determination than did the Federals to this attack. But they met intrenched infantry, and the concentrated fire of musketry, canister, grapeshot and shell mowed them down at every step. Yet they still struggled forward, but every Confederate stood at his post, and in a short time it was more than mortals could stand and they broke and fled, leaving eight hundred of their dead. The Thirteenth and One Hundred and Fifty-fourth were in the angle, supported on the right and left by the veterans of the Army of Tennessee.

While occupying this point the writer received orders from headquarters that the safety of the army depended upon holding this position, and that it must be held if it required the sacrifice of every man in the regiments. This order was communicated to the men and their unanimous response was that "we will stay here." A few days after this the army fell back and took position twelve miles below Marietta, Ga., at Vining station on the railroad to Atlanta. It was at this point, on the fourth day of July, 1864, while the regiment and brigade were resting in the trenches behind a battery that the writer lost a leg by the explosion of a shell from the enemy's battery, which released him from field service during the remainder of the war. Hence I had no personal knowledge of the movements of my old command after this date.

In a short time after this, Colonel George W. Gordon, of the Eleventh Tennessee, was promoted to Brigadier-General and took command of the brigade. The Thirteenth and One Hundred and Fifty-fourth Regiments were under his command at the crossing of Chattahoochee, at Peach Tree Creek, with Hardee on the twenty-second of July, in the defenses of Atlanta, at Jonesboro, at the capture of Dalton, at Spring Hill, at the bloody battle of Franklin, in front of Nashville, in the retreat out of Tennessee, and at Bentonville, N. C., the last battle of the war. From Belmont, Mo., the first engagement, to Bentonville, N. C., the last, this regiment shed luster upon the soldiery of Tennessee, and well merited the compliment of General Joseph E. Johnston when he said: "They were unsurpassed by the Old Guard of Napoleon, or the army that Wellington marched out of Spain into France."

When the great soldier and leader, Joseph E. Johnston, surrendered the remnant of the Army of Tennessee, on April 26, 1865, there were left of the gallant old Thirteenth less than fifty officers and men. More than twelve hundred men had once mustered in its ranks. Throughout the four years they had fallen in battle, been stricken in camp, died on the march, and sometimes, alas! in prison. Faithful always, only a handful were left when the curtain was rung down on the awful drama. I was not there to see the old flag furled, the guns grounded, and the swords handed over; but I know that the same heroism, fortitude and love were with the remnant, as had been with those who four years before had marched away from home at the call of country and of duty.

GENERAL A. J. VAUGHAN. 1885.

ROSTER OF OFFICERS OF The Thirteenth Regiment, TENNESSEE INFANTRY, C. S. A.

FIELD AND STAFF.

Capt. Jno. V. Wright. Elected Colonel at organization of the regiment; fought in the battle of Belmont; elected to the Confederate Congress, and resigned; Washington, D. C.

Capt. A. J. Vaughan. Elected Lieutenant-Colonel at organization of the regiment; elected Colonel on resignation of Col. Wright; re-elected Colonel at reorganization of the army at Corinth; promoted to Brigadier-General after the battle of Chickamauga; lost a leg at Vining station, below Marietta, Ga., on July 4, 1864; Memphis, Tenn.

Capt. W. E. Winfield. Elected Major at organization of the regiment; was in the battles of Belmont and Shiloh; resigned at reorganization of the army at Corinth; died since the war.

Lieut. W. E. Morgan. Appointed Adjutant at organization of the regiment; elected Lieutenant-Colonel after the battle of Belmont; re- elected Lieutenant-Colonel at reorganization of the army at Corinth; was killed at Murfreesboro.

Lieut. R. M. Harwell. Appointed Adjutant of the regiment after the battle of Belmont; re-elected Adjutant at reorganization of the army at Corinth; appointed Aid-de-Camp to Gen. Vaughan; painfully wounded at Shiloh; died in service.

T. B. Yancey. Company E; appointed Lieutenant in the regular C. S. Army; assigned to duty with Col. A. J. Vaughan, and, when he was promoted, was appointed on his staff; was wounded at Shiloh; postoffice, Somerville, Tenn.

T. P. Cole. Company H; appointed Sergeant-Major at organization of the regiment; elected Major at reorganization of the army at Corinth; killed at the battle of Murfreesboro.

W. Ed. Dyer. Appointed Regimental Commissary at the organization of the regiment; transferred to Gen. J. P. McGowan's Brigade; promoted to

Major; died since the war.

L. B. Cabler. Company A; appointed Regimental Quartermaster at organization of the regiment; resigned at reorganization of army at Corinth; died since the war.

W. D. F. Hafford. Appointed Chaplain at organization of the regiment; resigned; died since the war.

Leonard H. Milliken. Appointed Chaplain after W. D. F. Hafford resigned; appointed Brigade Chaplain; died since the war.

B. L. Dyer. Company E; elected Lieutenant at organization of the company; promoted to Captain; appointed Regimental Quartermaster; promoted to Brigade Quartermaster; promoted to Lieutenant-Colonel and Colonel; appointed Inspector on Gen. Vaughan's staff; wounded twice; died since the war.

Wm. J. Brown. Company E; appointed Assistant Commissary; promoted to Regimental Commissary; transferred to cavalry; Collierville, Tenn.

N. F. Harrison. Company C; appointed Sergeant-Major at reorganization of the army at Corinth; promoted to Lieutenant after the battle of Chickamauga; was wounded at Chickamauga; Germantown, Tenn.

W. A. Milliken. Company G; appointed Sergeant-Major after the battle of Chickamauga; Washington, D. C.

MEDICAL STAFF.

Dr. J. A. Forbes. Regimental Surgeon at organization of the regiment; resigned; went to the Virginia army.

Dr. Robt. W. Mitchell. Assistant Surgeon of Fifteenth Tennessee Regiment; appointed Surgeon C. S. A., October 1, 1861, and assigned to the Thirteenth Tennessee Regiment by seniority; Brigade Surgeon and Division Surgeon of Clark's Division; Memphis, Tenn.

B. F. Dickerson. Company I; elected Assistant Surgeon of Thirteenth Regiment; appointed Surgeon C. S. A. and assigned to Thirteenth Regiment; died since war.

N. M. Bostwick. Appointed Assistant Surgeon while a member of Company K, One Hundred and Fifty-fourth Senior Tennessee Regiment; assigned to duty in the Thirteenth Tennessee Regiment; seriously wounded in the foot near Lovejoy station and sent to hospital; Memphis, Tenn.

REGIMENTAL BAND AND INFIRMARY CORPS.

(Afterward Brigade Band.)

J. T. Ferth (leader), Memphis, Tenn.

T. E. Daily, Company H, wounded at the battle of Murfreesboro; Memphis, Tenn.

W. P. Lipscomb, Company G, LaGrange, Tenn.

W. F. Gowan, Company H, Bartlett, Tenn.

J. G. Leach, Company G, Holly Springs, Miss.

S. H. Lockhart, Company G, died since the war.

W. M. Herndon, Company L, died since the war.

R. P. White, Company G, Holly Springs, Miss.

J. E. Yancey, Company G, died since the war.

George Turner (drummer), One Hundred and Fifty-fourth Regiment, died since the war.

Mike Lynch, One Hundred and Fifty-fourth Regiment, died since the war.

Chas. E. McNamee, Company L, died in service.

J. H. Mitchell, Company G.

Hiram Richmond, Company C.

J. R. Millen.

Roster of Company A.

Arnold, T. H. Elected Second Lieutenant at organization of company; elected Captain after battle of Belmont; wounded at Belmont; resigned and joined cavalry; Memphis, Tenn.

Amis, S. S.

Burton, Wm. C. Elected Captain at organization of company; resigned after the battle of Belmont; died during the war.

Bell, W. A. Elected Third Lieutenant at Columbus, Ky.; resigned at the reorganization at Corinth; wounded at Shiloh; joined Twelfth Tennessee Cavalry; died since the war.

Brown, J. Fisherville, Tenn.

Baldridge, Wes. In Arkansas.

Blankinship, H.

Boyd, M. Died in service.

Beard, R. Discharged at Columbus, Ky., 1861.

Bone, Charley.

Bone, Church. Fourth Corporal.

Brooks, James.

Branch, P. Discharged at Columbus, Ky.

Burtin, —. Whiteville, Tenn.

Brown, Frank. Discharged at Columbus, Ky.

Clay, G. W. Transferred to cavalry.

Canada, J. M. Died since the war.

Carter, Fletcher. Elected Lieutenant; promoted to Captain at Chickamauga; killed at Franklin.

Claxton, E. A. Discharged at Corinth.

Claxton, W. W. Killed at Peach Tree Creek.

Crawford, W. E. Wounded at Shiloh and at Jonesboro; captured at Missionary Ridge; elected Lieutenant at Chickamauga; Somerville, Tenn.

Cabler, L. B. Appointed Regimental Quartermaster at organization of regiment; resigned at the reorganization of the army at Corinth; died since the war.

Crawford, P. D.

Cairy, C. M. Died in service at Chattanooga, Oct. 10, 1862.

Claxton, T. J. Died since the war.

Casey, J. N.

Crawley, Jim. Discharged at Corinth.

Cody, J. F. Wounded at Belmont; died in service.

Cain, Daniel. Killed in service.

Cody, M. Died since the war.

Carter, Burrus. Wounded at Belmont anddischarged.

Carter, J. Killed in service.

Donaldson, R. A. Killed in Richmond, Ky.

Duncan, W. C. Died in service, May 5, 1862.

Durham, H. Wounded at Shiloh; lost an eye; in Arkansas.

Daniel, T. Third Lieutenant; discharged 1863.

Eaton, B. F. Killed at Shiloh.

Eason, C. T. Discharged at Tupelo, 1862; died since the war.

Emmerson, J. L. Corporal; discharged at Columbus, Ky.; died since the war.

Edmondson, H. Fourth Sergeant.

Earles, J. K. Died since the war.

Fullerton, W. L. Killed at Richmond, Ky., Aug. 30, 1862.

Finney, W. P.

Frasier, G.

Frasier, Milt. Wounded at Belmont.

Frasier, Mark.

Goodbread, J. W. Died in service, 1861.

Godsey, W. H.

Gilliam, W. A. Wounded, Richmond, Ky.; died since war.

Goabey, J. M. Died since the war.

Gray, W.

Harris, Jim. Discharged, 1861.

Hunt, H. B. Killed at Shiloh.

Hexter, Jim. Killed at Belmont, or Shiloh.

Harrison, R. Killed at Shiloh.

Hickson, J. Discharged, 1862.

Hughbanks, —. Bolivar, Tenn.

Heflin, H. L. Wounded at Franklin in thigh and hand.

Harrison, R. K. Oakland.

Jones, J. Killed in service.

Jordan, Hardy. Died in service, June, 1862.

Kelley, J. C. Killed at Murfreesboro.

Kelley, P. M. Died in service, November, 1862.

Laurence, S. G. Killed at Richmond, Ky.

Langdon, James J. Wounded at Shiloh; elected Lieutenant at Chickamauga; detailed on recruiting service in Georgia; Moscow, Tenn.

Lockhart, A. H.

Moore, J. M. Killed at Shiloh.

Matmiller, Fred.

Middlemiss, A. First Sergeant; killed at Belmont.

Martin, James.

Moore, George. Wounded at Belmont and Atlanta, Ga.

Manus, J. D.

Moore, W. Died since the war.

Moore, James. Killed at Shiloh.

McCully, A. John. Killed at Belmont.

McCully, Miles. Killed at Belmont.

McCully, R. Died since the war.

Mathews, A. N. Killed at Shiloh.

Mathews, J. F. First Sergeant; elected Lieutenant at Corinth; wounded at Shiloh.

Morris, T.

Mathenting, Joe.

Manley, T.

Oliver, W. H.

Nobles, J. A. Died in service, May 17, 1864.

Poor, Thomas. Died in service, December, 1861.

Poor, E. H. Taken prisoner on Dallas campaign; Williston.

Pathon, George. Died in service at Tupelo, Miss.

Park, R. H. Died in service at Tupelo, Miss.

Pierce, J. Killed in Somerville, 1862.

Price, James.

Poston, Frank. Died in service, December, 1861.

Rankin, W. L. Died in service, May 28, 1862.

Rhea, Mathew. Elected First Lieutenant at organization of his company; killed at Belmont.

Roberson, J. W. Killed in battle.

Reardon, Wm. Captured at Belmont; he was never afterward with his company.

Roberts, —. Discharged at Corinth.

Roberts, J. M.

Reeves, Calvin J. Died in service, March, 1862.

Simon, John. Discharged at Corinth.

Shaw, W. J. Died in service, June 15, 1862.

Stephens, W. J. Killed at Chickamauga.

Shaw, J. C. Transferred to Sixth Tennessee Regiment; killed at Atlanta.

Stephens, W. D. In Arkansas.

Shay, Dan. Discharged at Dalton, Ga.

Simons, Thomas. Discharged at Corinth.

Stafford, W. Died in service, November, 1861.

Stafford, J. T.

Stafford, J. B. Died since the war.

Stafford, P. Oakland, Tenn.

Thompson, R. M. Killed at Shiloh.

Tucker, W. C. Died in service in Kentucky.

Taylor, Wm. Died since the war.

Thomas, G. Discharged, 1861.

Thompson, R. Killed at Shiloh.

Waggoner, J. L. Oakland, Tenn.

Wiley, D. C. Smithfield, Texas.

Williams, D. H. Wounded at Shiloh, again in 1864.

Webb, James.

Ward, W. P. In Texas.

Ward, Ed. Died in service, May, 1862.

Whitmore, C. H. Elected First Lieutenant; killed at Shiloh.

Ward, P. Died in service.

Wilson, W. P. Somerville, Tenn.

Williams, W.

Wilson, W. B. In insane asylum.

Walls, John.

Wilkerson, John.

Wilkerson, W. D. Transferred to Sixth Tennessee Regiment at Randolph; Memphis, Tenn.

Wilkerson, W. N. Memphis.

Wilson, J. E. Transferred to Company G; Williston, Tenn.

Note—Companies A and D were consolidated at the reorganization of the army at Corinth, and sometimes the names of killed and wounded are reported on both rosters.

Roster of Company B.

Adams, G. H. Killed atMurfreesboro.

Alexander, J. A. Died since the war.

Alexander, W. J. Wounded at Shiloh and Murfreesboro; when the color bearer was killed at Shiloh, he snatched up the flag and carried it until wounded; postoffice, Hickory Withe, Tenn.

Alexander, J. V. Wounded at Murfreesboro; postoffice, Oakland, Tenn.

Anderson, J. W. Died in service.

Askew, Benj. F. Wounded at Murfreesboro; postoffice, Hickory Withe, Tenn.

Burnett, W. H. Corporal; killed at Belmont.

Beal, T. S. Postoffice, Macon, Tenn.

Barron, J. T. Died in service December, 1863.

Barron, W. J. Promoted to Assistant Surgeon. Eleventh Tennessee Regiment; postoffice, Macon, Tenn.

Bailey, J. G. Wounded at Murfreesboro; died since war.

Blaydes, J. G. Postoffice, Oakland, Tenn.

Babbitt, J. G. Killed at Shiloh.

Brown, A. H. Wounded at Murfreesboro; Vanndale, Ark.

Brammett, B. F.

Burnett, J. E. Postoffice, Moscow, Tenn.

Carter, J. J. Died since the war.

Carter, W. R. Killed at Murfreesboro.

Castles, J. T. Severely wounded at Murfreesboro; at hospital one month; taken to Camp Morton; exchanged August, 1863.

Cocke, H. C. In Texas.

Cocke, W. L. Wounded at Murfreesboro; Prescott, Ark.

Cogbill, W. H. Elected First Sergeant at reorganization of army; wounded at Peach Tree creek; Wynne, Ark.

Coleman, B. F. Wounded at Perryville; Camden, Ark.

Crawford, W. H. Wounded at Murfreesboro; died since the war.

Cartwright, J. G. Died since the war.

Cartwright, T. M. Postoffice, Oakland, Tenn.

Dougan, S. B. First Lieutenant; killed at Shiloh.

Daily, T. E. Wounded at Murfreesboro; member of the band and infirmary corps; Memphis, Tenn.

Daily, G. W. Wounded at Murfreesboro; Petitsville, Ala.

Deener, S. F. Died in service at Columbus, Miss., 1861.

Dillard, A. R. Captured at Shiloh; never heard from.

Dougan, J. W. Discharged; postoffice, Williston, Tenn.

Dobbins, T. E. Died in service.

Etherton, A. W. Wounded at Murfreesboro; St. Louis, Mo.

Edenton, J. C. Wounded at Murfreesboro; Macon, Tenn.

Elder, J. C. Died in service.

Farley, J. M. Wounded at Resaca; died since the war.

Folwell, J. H. Killed at Franklin.

Folwell, J. W. Died since the war.

Folwell, R. V. Killed at Peach Tree creek, Ga.

Gaither, G. A. Wounded at Chickamauga; postoffice, Williston, Tenn.

Gaither, T. F. Killed at Richmond, Ky., August 30, 1862.

Gaither, W. M. Williston, Tenn.

Gardner, J. M. Captured at Corinth; Cotton Plant, Ark.

Granbery, Capt. J. L. Elected Captain at organization of company; served in regiment twelve months; resigned and joined cavalry; postoffice, Collierville, Tenn.

Granberry, R. B. Killed at Kennesaw mountain.

Garvin, J. A. Postoffice, Moscow, Tenn.

Higgason, E. J. First Sergeant; wounded at Belmont; died since the war.

Hare, T. E. Elected Second Lieutenant at reorganization of the army;

severely wounded at Richmond, Ky.; postoffice, Nicholasville or Lexington, Ky.

Hewlett, J. C. Died since the war.

Hollowell, M. D. Discharged from service; postoffice, Collierville, Tenn.

Irby, R. W. Wounded at Murfreesboro; Macon, Tenn.

Kerr, Jno. B. Died since the war.

Kyle, W. D. Captured at Belmont; exchanged; severely wounded at Atlanta, unfitting him for further service; postoffice, McCrary, Ark.

Lightle, B. F. Fourth Sergeant; elected Captain at reorganization of the army; wounded at Murfreesboro; died since the war.

Lazenby, T. W. Died in service.

Lightle, Richard. Killed by Kansas jayhawkers.

Little, Watt. Discharged from service.

Mebane, J. W. Third Lieutenant; transferred and elected Third Lieutenant in Wright's Battery; killed at Pine Mountain, Ga.

Mitchell, W. F. R. Elected Second Lieutenant at organization; died since the war.

Mathews, J. S. Captured at Kennesaw mountain, Ga.; Hickory Withe, Tenn.

Mewborn, J. L. Third Lieutenant; elected Third Lieutenant at reorganization; captured while on detail service and taken to prison; Memphis, Tenn.

Mewborn, J. C. Wounded at Murfreesboro; captured at Kennesaw mountain; Macon, Tenn.

Mewborn, J. W. Transferred from Company C; captured at Perryville and exchanged; wounded at Atlanta; postoffice, Macon, Tenn.

Mebane, Capt. W. G. Elected Captain at reorganization of army; wounded at Murfreesboro; captured at Kennesaw mountain; died since the war.

Mitchell, J. C. Died in service October, 1861.

Moore, J. L. Killed at Jonesboro, Ga.

Moore, Cadmus. Died since the war.

Murrell, A. R. Captured in 1864; died since the war.

McFerren, J. H. Second Sergeant; Collierville, Tenn.

McKinstry, J. Logan. Killed at Murfreesboro.

McLin, J. E. Discharged.

McClaren, F. M. Captured at Kennesaw mountain, Ga.; postoffice, Vanndale, Ark.

Neel, W. L. Discharged; died since the war.

Neel, T. V. Captured at Kennesaw; White Haven, Tenn.

Neel, S. M. First Corporal; wounded at Murfreesboro; Kansas City, Mo.

Owen, T. H. Hickory Withe, Tenn.

Owen, D. O. Discharged from service.

Parker, J. H.

Porter, W. B. Died in service.

Reid, W. B. Killed at Murfreesboro.

Reid, T. J. Promoted to Surgeon and assigned to Thirty-eighth Tennessee Regiment; died since the war.

Rhea, A. Promoted to Surgeon and assigned to post duty; postoffice, Whiteville, Tenn.

Richards, T. L.

Seward, A. N. Second Corporal; wounded at Murfreesboro; Hickory Withe, Tenn.

Steadman, W. C. Killed at Chickamauga.

Stone, W. T. Transferred from Company E to Company B; captured at Atlanta; died since the war.

Stone, Jake. Wounded at Murfreesboro; Florence, Ala.

Smith, J. P. Oakland, Tenn.

Sanderlen, J. W. Discharged from service; died since war.

Sanderlen, D. M. Captured, taken to prison, and died on his way home, after exchange.

Summers, J. Q. In Arkansas.

Summers, J. W. Coldwater, Miss.

Scott, J. M. Germantown.

Scott, Richard. Germantown.

Stockinger, F. M. Color Bearer; killed at Belmont.

Starks, T. J. Discharged from service.

Tomlinson, J. Wounded at Murfreesboro; postoffice, Williston, Tenn.

Tharp, J. C. Killed at Murfreesboro.

Torrence, J. T. Wounded at Richmond, Ky.; Moscow, Tenn.

Wade, W. P. Wounded at Murfreesboro; died since the war.

Ward, N. A. Killed at Atlanta, Ga.

Waller, E. M. Killed at Murfreesboro.

Warr, J. M. Transferred to Wright's Battery. Rossville, Tenn.

Willis, J. W. Died in service at Columbus, Ky.

Webber, J. T. Discharged from service; died since the war.

Walker, J. H. Killed at Shiloh.

Williams, B. M. Killed at Murfreesboro.

Williams, C. E. Died since the war.

Williams, J. H. Wounded at Murfreesboro; in Arkansas.

Williams, W. M. Elected Lieutenant at reorganization; wounded at Murfreesboro; died since the war.

Williams, W. J. Died in service at New Madrid, Aug. 4, '61.

Williams, T. J. Killed at Franklin.

Williams, W. W. Discharged from service.

Williams, John A. Wounded at Richmond, Ky.; killed at Franklin.

Roster of Company C.

Atkins, —.

Allison, Jim. Lieutenant.

Brooks, Henry. Lieutenant; killed at Missionary Ridge.

Buster, John. Died since the war.

Barsfield, J. W. Lebanon, Tenn.

Bettis, Tillman. Killed at Chickamauga.

Burton, Logan. Died in service, June 1, 1861.

Brackett, L. J. Died in service, June, 1862.

Carraway, Thomas. Lost an arm since the war; Memphis.

Crewson, Gus. Wounded at Franklin; died from wound.

Craig, Burt.

Cash, P. Boggan. Killed at Murfreesboro; only 18 years old; he wounded a Federal officer at Belmont, bound up his wounds, captured his sword and gave it to Gen. Marcus J. Wright, who sent it to his mother.

Douglass, H. F. Germantown.

Douglass, Elmore. Elected Lieutenant at organization of company; elected Captain at reorganization, and killed at Atlanta.

Dukes, Robert T. Killed at Murfreesboro.

Dukes, Wm. B. Killed at Shiloh.

Dunn, Laurence. Lost; supposed to have died.

Ellis, Wm. Captured; died in Alton prison.

Ellis, A. B. Wounded at Chickamauga and Missionary Ridge; Capleville.

Ellis, W. W. Wounded at Murfreesboro; paralyzed since the war; Capleville.

Elam, E. E. Was taken sick in Kentucky and left, but as soon as he was well enough joined the Eleventh Texas Cavalry and was crippled by the fall of a horse at Chickamauga; remained with the cavalry to the close of the war; Oakville.

Farrow, G. Ferd. Transferred to cavalry after Belmont.

Ford, Robt. Drowned after battle of Belmont; fell from boat.

Farrow, J. P. Killed at Belmont; fell at the first volley of the enemy.

Graham, C. P. Killed at Shiloh.

Gill, Wm. J. Tennessee.

Harrison, W. D. Elected to Lieutenant at organization of company; promoted to Captain on death of Capt. Douglass; Capleville.

Hutchinson, H. J. Killed at Shiloh.

Hilderbrand, John. Transferred to Wheeler's Cavalry; died since the war.

Holeman, Wayne. Killed at Murfreesboro, Dec. 31, 1862.

Hues, Andy. Died in service.

Herron, Louis. Transferred to cavalry; died since the war.

Harrison, N. F. Appointed Sergeant-Major at reorganization of the army at Corinth, 1862; promoted to Lieutenant after battle of Chickamauga; wounded at Chickamauga; Germantown.

Holeman, Tom, Jr. Wounded at Shiloh; Oakville, Tenn.

Harris, J. W. Killed at Belmont.

Jamison, J. P. Discharged for disability; died since war.

Jackson, Sam. Hernando, Miss.

Joplin, —.

Kyle, W. G. Died in service, May 17, 1862.

Kyle, Rogers. Texas.

Lake, W. L. Killed at Shiloh.

Lewis, Tobe.

Mitchell, John. Transferred to Sappers and Miners.

Morgan, W. E. Elected Lieutenant at organization of company; appointed Adjutant at organization of Thirteenth Regiment; elected Lieutenant-Colonel after battle of Belmont; re-elected Lieutenant-Colonel at reorganization of army at Corinth; killed at Murfreesboro; his name was inscribed on a piece of artillery as the most gallant officer of Cheatham's Division who fell on that battlefield.

Morgan, John. Elected Captain at organization of company; resigned at the reorganization of the army at Corinth; joined a Mississippi regiment; elected Captain; wounded at Belmont, and killed at Murfreesboro.

Madden, Jim. Clubbed his musket and struck a Federal soldier at Belmont, afterward lost an arm; died since the war.

Madden, George. Died in service.

McCarthy, Jim. Corporal.

McNichols, John. Wounded at Belmont and Shiloh; discharged after 12 months' service; died since the war.

Norris, N. Died since the war.

Nelson, W. Henry. Paralyzed since the war; Whitehaven.

Prest, Wm. Germantown.

Patterson, Joe A. Germantown.

Pittman, Arthur R. Killed atBelmont.

Paine, John. Died since the war.

Pierson, —.

Pratt, —.

Rogers, J. W. Killed at Belmont; his last words: "Tell my mother I died in discharging my duty; that was all I could do."

Rowlett, John W. Wounded at Murfreesboro; died since the war.

Rainy, Thomas, Color Bearer. Killed at Shiloh.

Rhodes, W. L. Killed at Richmond, Ky.

Richmond, Hiram. Died since the war.

Richmond, John. Died since the war.

Rickett, —.

Simms, Tim J. Wounded at Belmont; died from wounds.

Saffran, George.

Stratton, M. V. Wounded at Belmont and Missionary Ridge; captured at Franklin, but made his escape; Capleville.

Stratton, C. Died in service from wounds at Stone Mountain.

Stokes, W. L. Killed at Shiloh.

Sough, Jim. Killed in service.

Stratton, B. M. Wounded early in action at Shiloh; discharged; Memphis.

Stratton, J. H. Discharged for disability; joined cavalry.

Small, R. W. (Dick). Wounded at Belmont; twice captured and twice escaped; Hazen, Ark.

Seats, Wyatt.

Smith, John. Wounded at Murfreesboro.

Savage, John.

Shockly, —.

Tuggle, Joe. Killed at Peach Tree Creek, Ga.

Tuggle, Palmer B. Killed at Murfreesboro.

Tuggle, Thompson. Died in service at Columbus, Ky.

Tuggle, George R. Capleville.

Vandervest, —. Killed at Richmond, Ky.

Williams, J. H. Killed in service.

Williams, W. W. Wounded in service; died since the war.

Weatherall, A. C. Died since the war.

Walton, —.

Winford, Sam. Died since thewar.

Woodson, Gus.

Wright, John W. Wounded at Richmond, Ky., and at Murfreesboro and captured; Memphis, Tenn.

Roster of Company D.

Archibald, J. G. Died in service, June, 1861.

Bell, Frank. Yorkville, Tenn.

Biggs, Jeremiah, Yorkville, Tenn.

Brewster, R. S. Elected Captain on death of Capt. J. A. Wilkins; appointed Captain of Companies A and D at reorganization, and was in command at close of the war; Louisville, Ky.

Brewer, John A. Died in service in 1861.

Brewer, N. B. Died in service.

Busick, J. Morton. Kenton, Tenn.

Brown, Wm. Died since the war.

Burrus, John.

Cunningham, J. W. Elected Lieutenant at organization of company; died in service, May, 1862.

Carter, A. S.

Canada, Henry. Died since the war.

Canada, James. Wounded at Shiloh; Arkansas.

Gary, C. M. Died in service, September, 1862.

Carmack, Tip. Died in service.

Cowan, W. F. Elected Lieutenant at organization of the company; died from exposure in the battle of Shiloh.

Davis, Wm. Gleason, Tenn.

Dickey, A. J. Died since the war.

Dickey, James. Dyer county.

Dozier, B. M. Killed at Belmont.

Dozier, Joseph. Dyer county.

Duncan, W. C. Died in hospital in Mississippi, June, 1862.

Eaton, R. D. Killed at Shiloh.

Fullerton, Henry T. Shot through thigh, severing sciatic artery;

discharged at Shelbyville; Kenton, Tenn.

Fullerton, W. L. Killed at Richmond, Ky.

Garrison, Ed. Texas.

Gibson, Allen. Rutherford, Tenn.

Goodloe, C. A. Alamo, Tenn.

Goodloe, Morris. Transferred to cavalry; elected Lieutenant of cavalry under Forrest.

Greer, J. N. Died since the war.

Guthrie, Ewing. Missouri.

Hall, John R. Yorkville, Tenn.

Hale, James K. Polk. Yorkville, Tenn.

Hamilton, Robert, Died since the war.

Hinson, Ben. Yorkville, Tenn.

Holmes, Elihu. Elected Lieutenant; wounded at Belmont; died since the war.

Holt, Joseph. Newbern, Tenn.

Holt, James. Newbern, Tenn.

Hunt, H. B. Killed at Shiloh.

Jones, Charles. Died since the war.

Lee, James. Rutherford, Tenn.

Leigh, Wm. Died since the war.

Lawrence, James J. Killed at Richmond, Ky.

McCorkle, J. E. Elected Lieutenant at organization of company; resigned from bad health; Newbern, Tenn.

McCorkle, J. S. Newbern, Tenn.

McCorkle, Locke. Killed or died in service.

McCorkle, E. J. Died in service, August, 1862.

Mills, Eugene. Died in service.

Mathews, Elisha.

Minton, W. H. Killed at Richmond, Ky.

Minton, J. S. Died in service, June,1861.

Moore, T. Jeff. Winchester, Tenn.

Montgomery, John M. Discharged from ill-health; died since the war.

Montgomery, G. R. Died in service, 1861.

Northern, John B. Died since the war.

Northern, Rufus. Died in service.

Oakey, Mack. Died since the war.

Parks, Robert H. Died in service,1862.

Parks, W. H. Killed at Belmont.

Patton, Geo. W. Wounded at Shiloh; died in camp at Tupelo, 1862.

Penn, H. T. Christian county, Ky.

Pierce, Wm. Died either in service or at close of the war.

Polk, W. H. Killed at Belmont.

Ray, Alexander. Died since the war.

Rankin, W. D. Died in service, May, 1862.

Reed, John L. Yorkville, Tenn.

Roach, Harwood. Killed at Belmont.

Reynolds, Wm.

Robinson, J. H. Trenton, Tenn.

Robinson, W. P. Wounded at Belmont; Eaton, Tenn.

Robinson, M. R. Texas.

Robinson, John. Died in service from wounds in battle.

Scott, W. L. Died since the war.

Shaw, Wm. Died in service, June, 1862.

Shaw, John H. Killed at Belmont.

Senter, David. Trenton, Tenn.

Tucker, Wm. Died in service, October, 1862.

Wade, Nash. Texas.

Weddington, Rufus H. Wounded at Shiloh; Arkansas.

Wherry, L. C. Died in service.

Wilkins, J. A. Elected Captain at organization of company; killed at Shiloh.

Zaricor, Albert G. Killed at Belmont.

Roster of Company E,

Composed of Tennesseans and Mississippians.

Allen, Thos. B. Elected Lieutenant at organization of company; served 12 months; resigned; died since the war.

Allen, G. W. McKenzie, Texas.

Arnett, D. C. Killed at Shiloh; from Mississippi.

Arnett, R. C. Canaan, Miss.; from Mississippi.

Allen, Sam H. Wounded at Shiloh; Memphis, Tenn.

Abernathy, W. A. When the war broke out he was at Charlotte Military Institute; joined the First North Carolina Regiment; fought the battle of Big Bethel; was complimented by his officers for gallantry; was transferred to Company E, Thirteenth Tennessee Regiment; killed at Murfreesboro.

Brown, W. J. Appointed Commissary Sergeant of the regiment; transferred after the battle of Chickamauga to Forrest's Cavalry; wounded at Columbia, Tenn.; Collierville, Tenn.

Brown, A. C. Enlisted at Murfreesboro; wounded by the explosion of a shell, from which he never recovered, and is now in the asylum.

Bull, D. C. Killed at Shiloh.

Bailey, B. T.

Ballard, F. M. Missing at the battle of Richmond, Ky.; supposed to have been killed.

Batte, Tom B. Died in service.

Black, J. C. Killed at Shiloh; from Mississippi.

Blackwell, J. W. Transferred to a Georgia regiment; from Mississippi.

Bonner, R. H. Though not a member of Company E, he fought with it in the battle of Shiloh, and afterward became one of Henderson's famous scouts.

Boyd, J. W. Died since the war.

Bryan, J. D.

Burton, Cornelius. Killed on Kennesaw line.

Clay, L. B.

Cowan, James. Died in service, May 1, 1862.

Clay, W. C.

Craddock, Geo. C. Elected First Lieutenant; transferred to cavalry; killed at Nashville, Tenn.

Dyer, B. L. Elected Lieutenant at organization of company; promoted to Captain; appointed Quartermaster of regiment; promoted to Lieutenant-Colonel and Colonel of regiment; wounded at Vining Station and in front of Atlanta; Inspector-General on General Vaughan's staff; died since the war.

Dyer, M. B. Died since the war.

Davis, W. F. Died since the war; from Mississippi.

Davis, J. S. From Mississippi.

DeAregan, Dr. Assistant Hospital Surgeon of the regiment; died since the war.

Doyle, E. T. Canaan, Miss.; from Mississippi.

Doyle, Z. Q. Bride, Tenn.; from Mississippi.

Dennis, Charles. Died since the war; from Mississippi.

Dukes, W. A. Died in service, March 25, 1862.

Doyle, O. A. Died in service; from Mississippi.

Fuiks, Morris. Missing at Missionary Ridge; supposed to have been killed.

Fletcher, Asbury. Died since the war.

Forbes, J. A. Started out in Company E; was appointed Surgeon; resigned and went to Virginia army.

Green, A. J. Texas.

Green, Wm. Killed at Murfreesboro.

Gates, W. A.

Grissum, Felix; died since the war.

Grissum, M. C. Killed at Shiloh.

Grider, W. L.

Gober, B. W. Moscow, Tenn.

Gober, S.

Harwell, Richard M. Elected Lieutenant at organization of company; appointed Adjutant of the regiment; re-elected Adjutant at reorganization of the army at Corinth; appointed Aid-de-Camp to Gen. Vaughan; painfully wounded at Shiloh; died in the service.

Hicks, Sam. Discharged in Kentucky.

Hicks, M. D. Died since the war.

Holliday, G. W. Died in service, November 1, 1861.

Hogan, D. H. Discharged in 1862.

Hill, E. E. Arkansas; from Mississippi.

Hill, L. H. Killed at Atlanta; from Mississippi.

Heflin, H. L. Stanton, Tenn.

Jackson, W. A. Died since the war; from Mississippi.

Jackson, Tom. Killed at Perryville.

King, B. Died in service.

Landreth, W.

Leverett, J. W. Died since the war.

Lane, Thomas M. Severely wounded at Murfreesboro; died since the war.

May, Powell. Elected Lieutenant at the reorganization of the army at Corinth; Clarendon, Ark.

Moore, J. B.

Mason, David H. Died at Murfreesboro from smallpox; was wounded in the ear.

McConnell, Charles. Rossville, Tenn.

Moody, John A. Elected Captain at the reorganization of the army at Corinth; wounded at Chickamauga and Franklin; Trinity, Texas.

McNeese, John. Killed in Hernando, Miss., since the war.

McKinley, Robert W. Died since the war.

Newby, E. W. Mortally wounded at Belmont; died in Memphis from wound.

Pierce, W. G. Died since the war.

Pierce, J. R. Moscow, Tenn.

Pickins, R. T. Transferred from Company E to Company G; Moscow, Tenn.

Rosser, W. B. Discharged during war; Cotton Plant, Ark.

Rosser, J. H. Cotton Plant, Ark.

Robertson, S. J. Killed at Belmont.

Robertson, Alfred. Died in service, October, 1861.

Roland, W. T. Canaan, Miss.; from Mississippi.

Reed, W. C. Fisherville, Tenn.

Scarborough, L. A. Wounded and lost his foot; Memphis.

Scarborough, J. G. Discharged; died since the war.

Smith, J. W. Transferred to cavalry; promoted to Colonel of Cavalry; Grand Junction, Tenn.

Stinson, W. W. Cornersville, Miss.

Stinson, Anderson.

Stone, W. T. Transferred to Company B, Thirteenth Tennessee Regiment; captured at Atlanta; died since war.

Stuart, H. Died since the war.

Smart, N. Z. Grand Junction, Tenn.; from Mississippi.

Spencer, W. T. Died since the war: from Mississippi.

Teague, B. F. Moscow, Tenn.

Tiller, G. R. Killed at Belmont.

Tiller, Tom H. Died since the war.

Vaughan, A. J. Elected Captain at organization of regiment; elected Lieutenant-Colonel at Columbus, Ky.; re-elected Colonel at reorganization of army at Corinth; promoted to Brigadier-General; lost a leg; Memphis, Tenn.

Watts, C. W. Died in service.

Wells, E. S. Wounded at Belmont and Missionary Ridge; Canaan, Miss.; from Mississippi.

Yancey, B. Transferred from Company C, Ninth Mississippi Regiment, to Company E, Thirteenth Tennessee Regiment; Clarendon, Ark.

Whitehorn, H. H.

Yancey, T. B. Appointed Lieutenant in the regular Confederate States Army; assigned to duty with Col. A. J. Vaughan, and when he was promoted was appointed on his staff; Somerville, Tenn.

Zellner, J. W. Transferred at the reorganization of the army at Corinth from Company H to Company E; wounded at Shiloh, at Richmond, Ky., at Chickamauga and at Atlanta; Arlington, Tenn.

Roster of Company F.

Atkins, J. P. Wounded at Shiloh; Corinth, Miss.

Burns, M. N. Killed at Murfreesboro.

Barnett, H. H. Killed at Belmont.

Bell, Robert N. Detailed to drive Gen. Cheatham's headquarters wagon.

Cross, Richard. Captured at Belmont; died in service.

Connors, John. Died in service.

Cain, Dennis. Died since the war.

Churchwell, George W. Elected Captain at reorganization at Corinth; killed at Murfreesboro.

Clayton, Francis. Montezuma, Tenn.

Denchy, M. Killed at Shiloh.

English, W. E. Died in service, August 10, 1862.

Gullett, J. P. Died in service, March 1, 1862.

Guthrie, J. N. Killed at Shiloh.

Gorman, Dan. Severely wounded at Shiloh; Jackson, Tenn.

Hunt, Campbell.

Houston, A. K. Though not a member of this company, fought with it at Belmont; died since the war.

Hill, E. H. Killed at Belmont.

Henry, Samuel W. Elected First Lieutenant at organization; died in service first year of the war.

Houston, J. T. Corinth, Miss.

Hunt, E. C.

Isbell, S. M. Died in service, May, 1862.

Jones, —.

Jones, John A., Sr. Killed at Belmont.

Jones, John A., Jr. Killed at Belmont.

Johnson, J. R. Elected Lieutenant; died since the war.

Middleton, C. H. Killed at Belmont.

Morgan, John. Killed at Shiloh.

McGhee, J. F. Died in service, October, 1862.

McHughes, J. F. Died in service, October, 1862.

Owens, Enoch. Died in service.

Pinkston, Harrison. Elected Second Lieutenant; Colorado City, Texas.

Ramey, W. A. Orderly Sergeant; wounded in battle; Ark.

Sims, J. A. L. Died in service from measles, July, 1861.

Saunders, Wm. Killed at Shiloh.

Springer, J. D. Killed at Shiloh.

Shelby, James. Wounded at Shiloh; Texas.

Simms, Ezekiel. Madison county.

Simms, Milton. Captured and died during the war.

Thomas, B. L. Killed at Shiloh.

Wisdom, Dew M. Elected Lieutenant at organization of company; promoted to Captain after battle of Belmont; wounded twice at Belmont; resigned at reorganization of the army; went into cavalry; was made colonel of a cavalry regiment and served in Forrest's command till the close of the war; Guthrie, I. T.

Wigley, James. Died in service, August, 1861.

Winningham, H. L. Killed at Richmond, Ky.

Wiley, —. Died in service at Fort Wright, Memphis.

Williams, J. E. Died in service, June, 1862.

Yancy, J. E. Died in service, November, 1862.

Yarbro, Martin. Mortally wounded and died at Franklin, Tenn.

Wright, John V. Elected Captain at organization of the company; elected Colonel at organization of the regiment; fought at the battle of Belmont; elected to Confederate Congress; resigned; Washington, D. C.

Roster of Company G.

Adkins, —.

Baugh, Wm. Died since the war.

Baugh, Jno. Died since the war.

Boyd, Wm. Died since the war.

Burton, Cornelius.

Bidwell, A. W.

Brown, J. H. Killed at Shiloh.

Brewster, H. J. Died since the war.

Bennett, P. N. D. Killed at Belmont.

Bryant, R. C. Died since the war.

Burton, John W.

Baugh, Link. Died since the war.

Bickers, Wm. Died since the war.

Branscomb, Geo. Discharged; died since the war.

Cabler, Tom F. Died since the war.

Carraway, E. W. Fayette county.

Chapman, Walter C. Mississippi.

Connor, Chas. Died November 12, 1862.

Crenshaw, C. W.

Crenshaw, Terrell.

Dicks, Ed. Killed at Richmond, Ky.

Clay, L. B. Georgia.

Davis, Elijah. Died since the war.

Davis, Tom.

Donahue, Mike. Ordnance Sergeant.

Dyer, W. E. Appointed Regimental Commissary at organization of the company; transferred to Gen. J. P. McCown's Brigade; promoted to

Major; died since war.

Dowdy, John. Fayette county.

Edwards, Joe B. Wounded at Murfreesboro; died from the effects of the wound since the war.

Edwards, Warren. Texas.

Edwards. Tucker. Transferred to cavalry.

Ferth, J. T. Leader of the band and on infirmary corps.

Falls, Henry N. Commissary Sergeant; died since war.

Falls, Charley.

Gloster, Otey. Killed at Murfreesboro.

Gorman. E. W. Wounded at Jonesboro; captured and exchanged; wounded at Nashville; Germantown, Tenn.

Gynne, Steve J. Killed after the war.

Gynne, Henry C. Moscow, Tenn.

Gynne, Gus. Died since the war.

Gynne, H. L. Texas.

Heath, Z. W. Entered service at age of 15; arm shattered at Richmond, Ky.; badly wounded at Atlanta, which disabled him for further service; paroled from convalescent camp; Terrell, Tex.

Huddleston, W. H. Bolivar, Tenn.

Herndon, W. M. Member of band and on infirmary corps.

Henderson, Sam. Died since the war.

Jobert, Lee. Color Bearer; killed at Missionary Ridge.

Jones, John W. Killed at Murfreesboro.

Jones, Wiley F. Transferred to cavalry; LaGrange, Tenn.

Jones, Arthur. Memphis, Tenn.

Jones, J. A. Died in service, June 15, 1861.

Jones, Paul.

Kane, A. C. California.

Lashley, Jim. Elected Lieutenant at organization of company; resigned; died during the war.

Lacey, W. C.

Lanier, R. F. Elected Lieutenant at organization of company; promoted to Captain; severely wounded, from which he never recovered; died since the war.

Lanier, Ed. Elected Lieutenant at organization of company; killed at the battle of Richmond, Ky.

Lipscomb, Geo. LaGrange, Tenn.

Lipscomb, Peter. Member of band and on infirmary corps; LaGrange, Tenn.

Leach, Josh G. Member of band and on infirmary corps, Holly Springs.

Landrum, L. Killed at Columbus, Ky., after the war.

Limburger, W. C. Known as "Blind Tiger;" Greenville, Tex.

Moorman, H. C. Elected Lieutenant; Somerville, Tenn.

Moorman, Robert A. Killed atFranklin.

Massey, Nat. Discharged; died.

Mitchell, James. Big Greasy.

Mitchell, J. H. Died in service at Cleveland, Tenn.

Mustin, J. M. Died in service at Chattanooga, June 22, '63.

Mayo, John. Killed at Belmont.

Malone, Lon. Died since the war.

Malone, Cass.

McKnight, John. Forrest City, Ark.

McNamee, John T. Lieutenant; detailed on special duty; killed in the discharge of his duty in Fayette county.

McNamee, W. T. Wounded in service; died since war.

McKinstry, M. M. Killed at Shiloh.

McNeel, J. J. LaGrange, Tenn.

Palmer, Chas. Elected Lieutenant at organization of company; resigned; died during or since the war.

Parham, W. R. Joined company after battle of Shiloh; slightly wounded at Murfreesboro and on the Dalton campaign; Holly Springs, Miss.

Penn, John. Killed at Belmont.

Pickins, R. T. Transferred from Company E to Company G; Moscow, Tenn.

Price, Will.

Parham, Walter.

Parham, W. S. Died in service.

Parham, Frank.

Parham, Josh. O. Forrest City, Ark.

Parham, Joshua. Died in service.

Pledge, Clinton.

Rainey, John H. Alabama.

Rawlings, Joe. Killed at Franklin.

Rieves, Mat.

Rodgers, W. J. Elected Lieutenant; Moscow, Tenn.

Robertson, Jim F. Died in service.

Reeves, J. M.

Reeves, Will H. Died since the war.

Sturdevant, Jim.

Sharp, Rufus. Transferred to pioneer corps.

Sigman, T. F. Holly Springs, Miss.

Simmons, Rufus.

Stewart, M. Don. Died in service at Columbus, Ky.

Sullivan, Jim. Died at Tupelo, Miss., 1862.

Simmons, W. H. Killed at Murfreesboro.

Stafford, Noah. Wounded at Shiloh.

Steger, Jno. J. Discharged on account of his eyes; afterward joined the cavalry; captured at Holly Springs and sent to Irving Block; released and returned to his company; paroled with army at Greensboro, N. C.

Todd, J. R. Died since the war.

Tucker, R. G. Wounded at Shiloh; LaGrange, Tenn.

Thornton, W. S. Wounded in service; died since the war.

Taylor, Will. Wounded at Kingston, Ga.; discharged on account of his wound; died.

Winfield, W. E. Elected Captain at organization of company; elected Major at organization of regiment; was in the battles of Belmont and Shiloh; resigned; died since the war.

Winston, T. J. Killed by fall of horse since the war.

Winfield, J. O. Killed at Shiloh.

Winston, Jim.

Woodard, B. T. Transferred to Forrest's Cavalry.

Whyte, R. P. Member of band and on infirmary corps; Holly Springs, Miss.

Weems, John. Teamster.

Winston, Ed. Middle Tennessee.

Woods, E. O. Lieutenant; died since the war.

Wilson, J. E. Transferred from Company A; Williston.

Young, Dave. Middle Tennessee.

Yancey, Frank. Severely wounded at Murfreesboro; Memphis.

Yancey, Jas. E. Member of band and on infirmary corps; died since the war.

Roster of Company H.

Allen, J. W. Wounded severely at Murfreesboro; Dexter, Tenn.

Allen, Ed. Died since the war.

Aiken, Sam Dudley. Wounded at Belmont; killed at Murfreesboro.

Aiken, W. M. Captured at Peach Tree Creek and sent to Camp Chase.

Anderson, J. W. Killed at Adairsville, Ga.

Allen, Walter. Died since the war.

Barnes, William. Discharged.

Bond, W. A. Wounded at Atlanta.

Berryhill, Frank. Died since the war.

Bazimore, Thomas. Died in service.

Brown, Wilber. Died in service.

Bond, N. P. Died since the war.

Brooks, R. H. Wounded at Shiloh; White Station, Tenn.

Bond, R. B. Died in service, April 18, 1862.

Barber, Buck. Arkansas.

Bass, E. Died in service.

Chambers, J. F. Mississippi.

Chambers, T. J. Wounded at Peach Tree Creek; Tipton Co.

Chambers, E. O. Killed at Shiloh.

Claiborn, Wm. B. Killed at Richmond, Ky.

Cole, S. O. Killed at Shiloh.

Cole, R. A. Captured at Missionary Ridge; died in prison.

Cole, Jackson.

Coulter, W. S. Captured at Peach Tree Creek; Arkansas.

Coulter, Ben. Died in service, in hospital.

Cole, P. H. Appointed Sergeant-Major at organization of regiment; elected Major at reorganization of army at Corinth; killed at

Murfreesboro.

Christopher, L. Gainsboro, N. C.

Callis, Clem. Captured at Jonesboro and exchanged; Germantown.

Crouch, R. H. Killed at Richmond, Ky.

Craig, W. E. Died in service.

Clayton, Henry M. Died since the war.

Dunlap, D. R. Germantown.

Dunlap, Wm. J. Killed at Belmont.

Dailey, Ed. Elected First Lieutenant at organization of company; resigned; joined Forrest's Cavalry; killed at Sulphur Trestle.

Donelson, R. S. Wounded severely at Chickamauga; unfit for service the balance of the war; Arlington, Tenn.

Echlin, J. B. Captured at Murfreesboro; died in prison.

Ellis, P. S. Wounded at Shiloh; Lenow, Tenn.

Exum, W. H. Lieutenant; killed at Atlanta, Ga.

Easthorne, E. P. Died since the war.

Echles, George. Buntyn Station.

Farabee, B. F. First Sergeant; wounded and captured at Nashville; Memphis.

Finnegan, J. P.

Forgey, T. J. Killed at Murfreesboro.

Freeman, W. F. Transferred.

Ferguson, Thomas. Died since the war.

Garrett, John.

Goodloe, R. C. Died in service, September 30, 1861.

Gowan, Haywood. Harrison Station, Miss.

Gowan, W. F. Member of band and on infirmary corps; Bartlett, Tenn.

Goodlett, J. E. Elected Lieutenant; died in service.

Gray, Willis. Died since the war.

Griffin, Thomas. Killed while in service, by lightning.

Hall, Robt. G. Shot through both eyes at Franklin, Tenn.; entirely blind; Dexter, Tenn.

Hall, George. Killed at Belmont.

Hodge, John. Elected Lieutenant in a company of the Fifty-first Tennessee Regiment; transferred.

Hancock, John. Captured at Missionary Ridge; Red Banks, Miss.

Herring, Lon S. Elected Lieutenant; wounded at Shiloh; died since the war.

Jordan, G. S. Elected Lieutenant at organization of company; resigned for bad health in 1861; joined the Twelfth Tennessee Cavalry in Forrest's command; was detailed in the Quartermaster's Department with Neely's Brigade; Memphis, Tenn.

Lambe, James. Mississippi.

Land, John T. Near Brunswick, Tenn.

Loring, A. R. Died in service, November 14, 1864.

Lockridge, J. W. Wounded at Shiloh.

Lock, J. W. Wounded at Belmont; discharged on account of his age at Tupelo; joined Forrest's Cavalry; died since the war.

Lurray, A. W. Raleigh, Tenn.

Lenow, John H. Discharged; Memphis, Tenn.

Moore, A. J. Captured at Missionary Ridge; died since the war.

Munson, S. A. Elected Lieutenant; promoted to Captain; wounded at Shiloh; captured on Missionary Ridge and sent to prison at Johnson's Island; Memphis, Tenn.

Mullins, T. B. Mullins Station.

Moore, J. R. Died in service, June 8, 1862.

Marshall, W. A. Died October 8, 1861.

Mason, R. M. Elected Quartermaster at organization of the regiment; promoted to Depot Quartermaster by General Pillow at Columbus, and promoted to Corps Quartermaster by Gen. Polk; died since the war.

Miller, Lucius W.

Massey, J. W. Died in service, April 28, 1863.

McDonald, J. W. Transferred to marine service.

McBrooks, John. Detailed in the Quartermaster's Department, where he served during the war; died since war.

Nolly, W. B. Elected Lieutenant at organization of regiment; resigned in 1863 for bad health; Little Rock.

Nathan, Sam. Died in service.

Osborn, George. Arkansas.

Owens, W. G. Died in service.

Patrick, Henry. Discharged at Chickamauga, for disability and bad health. Lenow, Tenn.

Powell, C. W. Killed at Franklin.

Perkins, N. C. Elected Lieutenant at organization of company; resigned at Columbus in 1861; Memphis, Tenn.

Potts, Thomas J. Died in service.

Pittman, R. W. Elected Captain at organization of his company; wounded slightly at Belmont and severely at Shiloh; promoted to Lieutenant-Colonel on the death of Lieut.-Col. Morgan, and to Colonel of the regiment on the promotion of Col. Vaughan to Brigadier General; Denton, Tex.

Russell, J. W. Mortally wounded at Shiloh; died in service.

Roberts, William. Missing at Perryville, and was either killed or captured.

Rogers, Chip. Died since the war.

Rogers, Harvey. Died since the war.

Robinson, Henry. Color Corporal; missed at Richmond, Ky.; either killed or captured; most probably killed.

Royster, D. R. Killed at Shiloh.

Starr, Howard. Killed December 20, 1862.

Stephenson, J. J. Killed at Richmond, Ky.

Sensing, J. P. Bell, Tenn.

Sensing, Robert. Gadsden, Tenn.

Sweeney, Casey. Wounded at Franklin; died since the war.

Sturges, J. L. Morning Sun, Tenn. Snell,

J. T. Killed at Richmond, Ky. Snowden,

M. C. Died since the war. Timmons,

Henry. Buntyn Station, Tenn.

Thompson, J. A. Killed at Atlanta.

Turner, George W. Elected Lieutenant; killed in front of Atlanta on outpost duty.

Turner, J. W. Died since the war.

Turner, W. W. Died since the war.

Thompson, C. Virgil. Florida.

Tally, A. J. Wounded at Shiloh and died from wounds.

Terry, J. W.

Thomas, William. Died since the war.

Waddell, George. Died since the war.

Waddle, S. B. Arkansas.

Wooten, T. J. Wounded at Atlanta; permanently disabled; Eatonton, Ga.

Williams, J. Kimball. Died in service.

Wiley, Thomas. Elected Lieutenant.

Whitehead, J. W. Died since the war.

Wynne, George W. Covington, Tenn.

Woodson, Henry M. Transferred from Company E, Thirty-fourth Mississippi Regiment, to Company H, Thirteenth Tennessee Regiment; Memphis, Tenn.

White, W. F. Died since the war.

White, Dick. Died since the war.

Whitley, J. P. Arkansas.

Yates, Ed A. Wounded at Adairsville, Ga.; died since war.

Yates, P. C. Wounded at Murfreesboro and captured; Dexter, Tenn.

Yates, W. H. Wounded at Jonesboro; Dexter, Tenn.

Young, J. Carr. Killed at Shiloh.

Zellner, J. W. Transferred at reorganization to Company E; wounded at Shiloh, Richmond, Ky., Chickamauga, on New Hope Line and at Atlanta; Arlington, Tenn.

Roster of Company I.

Autry, John. Died in service, October 15,1861.

Alsup, Wm. Died in service, October 10, 1861.

Anderson, Andrew.

Barham, R. J., Jr. Wounded at Atlanta; died since the war.

Bray, B. M. Elected Second Lieutenant; wounded at Shiloh; Santiago, Cal.

Bray, Randolph. Mortally wounded at Richmond, Ky., and died.

Berger, G. W. Killed at Shiloh.

Bell, John. Died in service, August 1, 1861.

Beaver, W. H. Died in service, October 4, 1861.

Brewer, Jno. Died in service, Oct. 7, 1861, at Columbus, Ky.

Barham, Jno. Died in service, Oct. 10, 1861, atRandolph.

Baine, Bob. Mifflin, Tenn.

Baine, James. Texas.

Brown, Harper. Mifflin, Tenn.

Brown, W. J. Altus, Ark.

Barham, R. J., Sr. Wounded at Shiloh and Murfreesboro.

Barham, Richard. Drowned at Frankfort, Ky., 1862.

Barham, Isaiah. Wounded at Murfreesboro; transferred to Forrest's Cavalry; killed at Parker's Cross Roads.

Bailey, Thomas. Texas.

Crook, W. J. Started out private; elected Captain; promoted to Major Thirteenth Tennessee Regiment; died since the war.

Cawthon, James. Malden, Mo.

Crook, E. H. Henderson Station, Tenn.

Crook, W. B. Texas.

Croom, Ben. Pinson, Tenn.

Crow, G. W. Died in service just before battle of Murfreesboro, December 13, 1862.

Cawthon, Kit. Killed at Belmont.

Carver, Henry. Died in service, Sept. 11, 1861, atMemphis.

Collins, Nathan. Texas.

Crooms, James. Died in service in Mississippi in 1862.

Collins, J. F. Texas.

Crooms, Jesse. Pinson, Tenn.

Dickerson, B. F. Started out private; appointed Assistant Surgeon of Thirteenth Regiment; promoted to Surgeon of Thirteenth Regiment; died since the war.

Dickerson, W. B. Died in service, August 22, 1861.

Diffee, Clark. Wounded on infirmary corps at Shiloh; White Fern, Tenn.

Daniel, Thomas.

Dickie, Thomas. Died in service, 1862.

Daniels, "Parson." Mississippi.

Edwards, Wm. Third Lieutenant; McKinney, Texas.

Edwards, J. R. Mifflin, Tenn.

Fawcett, M. Texas.

Farrow, P. B. Died since the war.

Farnsworth, Wm. Wounded at New Hope Church.

Fringer, W. H. Died since the war.

Farnsworth, Sam. Died since the war.

Freeman, W. H. Lexington, Tenn.

Green, G. B. Killed at Murfreesboro.

Griswell, John.

Galbreath, J. N. Discharged during the war; Center Point, Tenn.

Glenn, Peter. Wounded at Murfreesboro; killed at Franklin.

Henry, Felix. Died in service.

Hendrix, J. C. Wounded at Shiloh; died in service at Oxford, Miss.

Hamlett, L. F. Killed at Belmont.

Hart, Thomas. Wounded at Belmont, Shiloh, Richmond, Ky., and at Atlanta; died since the war.

Hart, J. M. Transferred to Henderson's scouts; died since the war.

Haltom, B. F. Killed at Richmond, Ky.

Hart, James. Wounded July 22, 1864; died since the war.

Holis, Crow. Discharged before the battle of Richmond.

House, Freeman.

Hardeman, Joseph. Discharged during the war.

Hardeman, Newton. Discharged during the war.

Haltom, Elisha.

Houston, Wm. H. Pinson, Tenn.

Hurt, Jeremiah. Died in service, October 2, 1862.

Hamlett, Daniel. Died in service.

Hamlett, James. Killed at Belmont.

Hendrix, Jerry. Wounded at Murfreesboro, captured and died in prison.

Horton, L. D. Shady Hill, Tenn.

Horton, Jess. Shady Hill, Tenn.

Haygard, —. Henderson, Tenn.

Hubbard, John.

Ivey, James. Killed at Richmond, Ky.

Joiner, Arch. Wounded at Franklin; Mifflin, Tenn.

Joiner, Joe. Mifflin, Tenn.

Laird, T. B.

Mitchell, John. Killed at Shiloh.

Mitchell, Thomas. Died in service.

Milton, Wm. Discharged during thewar.

Mitchell, James. Mifflin, Tenn.

McHaney, C. F. Lexington, Tenn.

McGlothen, Joe. Dyer county. McGlothen,

John. Died in service. McLaughlin, J. H.

Killed at Murfreesboro.

McNeely, F. W. Died in service, April 2, 1862.

McCallum, Daniel. Killed at Atlanta.

Nesbit, John G. Killed at Belmont.

Neil, G. H. Died in service, June 1, 1862.

Neil, Sam. Morris Chapel, Tenn.

Ozier, G. B. Killed at Atlanta.

Ozier, J. D. Memphis, Tenn.

Ozier, John W. The first man wounded on skirmish line at Belmont; wounded at Shiloh, and at Franklin three times; Henderson, Tenn.

Parish, John. Wounded at Belmont and Franklin; Henderson, Tenn.

Priddy, Chas. W. Wounded at Belmont and lost right arm at Atlanta; died in service near close of the war.

Piles, A. B. Wounded at Belmont. Arkansas.

Purdy, John R. Florida.

Ross, G. L. Elected Captain at organization of company; served 12 months and resigned; died since the war.

Reed, John. Killed at Richmond, Ky.

Roberson, Lewis. Killed at Shiloh.

Rice, J. R. Elected Lieutenant; died since the war.

Rice, Frank. Died since the war.

Roberson, Winslow. Henderson, Tenn.

Ross, S. R. Wounded at Shiloh; Henderson, Tenn.

Rhodes, Jerry. Texas.

Smith, A. J. Died in service, at hospital in Mississippi.

Stone, R. R. Wounded at Shiloh; killed at Richmond, Ky.

Starnes, John.

Stewart, Wm. Lost a leg in service.

Stone, Ike A. Badly wounded in the head at Murfreesboro, yet he bound up his wounds and fought gallantly in every charge during the day; was complimented at Richmond, Ky., by Gens. E. Kirby Smith and Cleburne for gallant conduct on the field; was so badly wounded at Jonesboro that he has to this day to be moved about in a chair; Jack's Creek, Tenn.

Stone, W. C. Killed at Atlanta in a desperate charge; he crossed the enemy's works and fell, pierced by five balls.

Stegall, Jasper. St. Louis, Mo.

Stegall, M. J. Elected Third Lieutenant at Columbus, but had to resign for bad health; afterward joined Forrest's Cavalry; was captured and died in Alton prison.

Snow, R. D. Wounded at Murfreesboro, Dec. 30, 1862; also at Atlanta, August, 1864; Morris Chapel, Tenn.

Seemore, John. Died since the war.

Tillman, D. R. Killed at Murfreesboro.

Thompson, J. P. Henderson Station.

Thomas, Champ. Died since the war.

Vandike, J. N. Killed at Shiloh.

Vandike, A. M. Wounded at Shiloh in shoulder and then in right breast; Center Point, Tenn.

Wilson, N. B. Died in service, July 5, 1861.

Waggoner, H. N. Killed at Belmont.

Ward, Minous. Illinois.

Wheatly, Addy. Lexington, Tenn.

Wilson, Van. Mississippi.

Roster of Company K.

Aden, G. W. Wounded at Belmont.

Albritton, James H.

Anderson, L. W.

Baker, Henry W.

Brown, A. D. Sergeant; elected Lieutenant at reorganization; killed at the battle of Franklin.

Buchanan, Thomas C. First Sergeant; promoted to Lieutenant in 1861; wounded at Shiloh.

Bryant, John M.

Blankinship, C.

Brent, W. H. Died in service, February, 1862.

Burnham, Joshua.

Clany, Edwin S.

Chitwood, C. A. Killed at Shiloh.

Chrisman, J. H. Died in service, May, 1862.

Clark, James W.

Cole, James M.

Cross, Marcellus A.

Duke, Geo. T. Corporal; wounded at Shiloh.

Duke, James F. Killed at Murfreesboro.

DeBerry, N. E. Second Lieutenant; resigned on account of ill health; wounded at Belmont.

Essary, William J.

Espy, W. H.

Espy, Robt. R. Discharged in 1861.

Endaly, James T.

Fields, W. B. Sergeant; wounded at Belmont; discharged.

Featherston, W. V. Wounded at Shiloh.

Ferrell, Thomas H. Appointed Sergeant in 1862.

Forshell, Thomas V.

Ferrell, Sam A.

Fortner, Isaac.

Gibson, John W.

Gooch, Alex. Campbell. Died in Columbus Sept., 1861.

Hall, Julius M. Discharged, having furnished substitute.

Hall, Young W. Killed at Belmont.

Hall, William. Substituted for J. M. Hall.

Harden, W. C. Died in service, June, 1861.

Hebbits, Joseph R. Elected Captain at reorganization in 1862; transferred to Forrest's Cavalry, and killed at Cross Roads.

Holland, Joseph W. Discharged in 1862.

Howard, James L. Died in service in 1862.

Huffman, John A. Detailed as blacksmith in Government shop at Columbus, Ky.

Halbrook, W. H.

Kirk, M. R. Died in service, December, 1861.

Jones, Richard M.

Lemmett, Alfred.

Lalspeich, David. Detailed.

Lyons, W. J.

Latta, Sam'l R. Elected Captain at organization of company; resigned at reorganization of army at Corinth; wounded at Belmont.

McDavid, Sam'l. Second Sergeant.

Mays, Thomas S.

Madden, Jas. R. First Sergeant; died in service in 1862.

Pierce, Joseph A. Elected First Lieutenant at organization of the company.

Purcell, Joseph H. Elected Second Lieutenant December, 1861; wounded at Belmont.

Parish, J. A. Killed at Belmont.

Presgron, George W.

Pitts, Theophilus.

Prater, Frank. Died in service, January, 1861.

Richardson, Jno. Corporal; wounded at Belmont; elected Lieutenant at reorganization; killed at Franklin.

Robertson, Jesse R.

Robertson, George W.

Rush, William M.

Recroft, R. W.

Redding, Henry P. Died in service, November 20, 1861.

Saunders, James C.

Saunders, E. B. Wounded at Belmont.

Saunders, W. H.

Seats, William. Transferred to M. R. Hill's Regiment; elected Captain.

Sampson, Frank P. Elected Lieutenant; severely wounded in the Dalton campaign; died since the war.

Sengleterry, D. N.

Skipwith, Carter E. Killed at Murfreesboro.

Smith, N. I.

Smith, James Lowry. Killed at Belmont.

Shouthel, French M.

Scott, Thomas. Died in service in1861.

Skipper, James.

Tansell, John B. Corporal.

Tedford, James W. Wounded at Belmont.

Warren, N. W. Corporal.

Walker, S. B. Wounded at Belmont.

Weakley, W. B.

Williamson, J. K.

Wriley, Green.

Wilkerson, Felix.

Woods, S. D. Brevet Second Lieutenant; resigned on account of ill health.

Walker, James Archer. Died in service.

Walker, Washington L. Died in service, October, 1861.

Roster of Company L.

Acord, —.

Askew, John. Died since the war.

Askew, N. B. Died in service, November 11, 1862.

Anderson, M. L. Elected Lieutenant at Shelbyville, Tenn., in 1863; LaGrange, Tenn.

Arnitt, Dick. Died since the war.

Adkinson, Thomas. Killed at Atlanta.

Blakeslee, C. T. Wounded severely at Murfreesboro, which disabled him for field service, and was detailed in the commissary department; Hickory Flat.

Bass, R. J. Died during the war.

Bailey, R. J. Killed at the battle of Murfreesboro.

Booth, Joe. Living.

Batte, T. Died in service.

Booth, F. Near Somerville, Tenn.

Bennett, —. Killed at Murfreesboro.

Bennett, —. Living.

Collins, Samuel. Killed in service.

Collins, John.

Doyle, O. N. Died in service, August 15, 1862.

Ewell, Dr. A. C. Died in 1878.

Farmer, John. Died in service, May, 1862.

Finch, B. H. Died since the war.

Ferth, W. T. Died since the war.

Farris, Walsh. Living in Fayette county.

Gaugh, E. Died in service, December, 1862.

Gates, John H. Killed at Richmond, Ky.

Gordon, J. K. Died in service, January 1, 1863.

Gray, H. A. Killed at Richmond, Ky.

Gray, W. C. Captured and died in prison.

Gates, W. H. Elected Lieutenant at organization of company; killed at Murfreesboro.

Herndon, W. M. Member of the band and on infirmary corps; died since the war.

Hodges, C. T. Little Rock, Ark.

Jones, C. B. Elected Captain at organization of the company; severely wounded at Murfreesboro; resigned; died since the war.

Jenkins, J. S. Killed at Richmond, Ky.

Jenkins, S. T. Died in service, August 1,1862.

King, B. Died in service, May, 1862.

Lax, R. M. Hickory Valley.

Lloyd, T. P. Discharged in Kentucky for ill health.

Lane, Tom. Severely wounded; arm shattered; died of yellow fever in 1878.

McNamee, C. E. Wounded and died at Atlanta, Ga.

Milliken, W. A. Appointed Sergeant-Major after battle of Chickamauga; Washington City.

Milliken, L. H. Appointed Chaplain after resignation of W. D. F. Hafford; appointed Brigade Chaplain; died since the war.

Moody, R. E. Elected Captain to succeed C. B. Jones; died since the war.

Mason, David. Wounded in battle; died in service from smallpox at Murfreesboro.

Mason, Tom L. Seriously wounded in the foot at Atlanta; living in Mississippi.

Morton, Wm. M. Died since the war.

McCaskell, J. A. Died in service, August, 1862.

McCaskell, —. Died since the war.

McNeill, James A. Died since the war.

Malone, Ben. Living.

Oliver, John.

Pledge, Wm. A. Died in 1896.

Prewett, Mansfield. Grand Junction, Tenn.

Prewett, Jerry. Killed at Resaca, Ga.

Parham, Lee. Died since the war.

Parham, App. Wounded; died from wound.

Radford, John. Died since the war.

Sutherland, W. A. Killed after the war.

Shelton, Geo. P. Died in 1871.

Scott, Reuben. Elected Lieutenant at organization of the company.

Scott, Henry F. Died since the war.

Shenault, Isaac. Died in service.

Shenault, Joe. Tipton county.

Shenault, Walter. Died in service.

Sharp, John. Died in service, April 1, 1863.

Sims, B. G. Killed at Richmond, Ky.

Smart, John.

Smith, J. M. Killed at Missionary Ridge.

Ursery, John.

Ursery, —.

Waddell, Gray. Killed at Atlanta.

Waddell, J. D. Elected Lieutenant; living.

Wooten, Henry. Died in service at Knoxville, 1862.

Wooten, Joe. Died at the close of the war.

Winfield, M. R. Killed at Richmond, Ky.

Wilkerson, W. W. Died in service, May, 1862.

Wilkerson. B. W. Killed at Richmond, Ky.

Winston, Ed. Middle Tennessee.

Webster, B. Died in service, 1862.

Winfield, W. W. (Tish.) Discharged for ill health on surgeon's certificate; died since the war.

Faithful Colored Servants.

The survivors of the Thirteenth Regiment, like the writer, remember most gratefully the faithful body servants who followed us during the dark and bloody period. I have endeavored to collect the names of these colored men—slaves then, but freemen at the end—and add them here to this roster, believing as I do that their personal loyalty and faithful service entitle them to "honorable mention."

Roach Howard, Company E.
Berry Moore, Company E.
Joe Farrow, Company C.
Baltimore Tuggle, Company C.
Ike Mullins, Company H.
Dick Tuggle, Company C.
Dave Thompson, Company H.
Booker Hart, Company I.
Durell Bailey, Company B.
Granville Cash, Company B.
Ike Jamison, Company C.
Alf Ellis, Company C.
Kelsey Mebane, Company B.
Romeo Parham, Company G.
Sam Falls, Company G.
Mull Harrison, Company C.
Ike Payne, Company C.
Jack Mathes, Company B.
Orange Donelson, Company H.
Jack Farabee, Company H.
Arthur Ecklin, Company H.
Young Thurman, Fourth Tenn. Regt.
Henry Morgan, Company C.
Jack Dyer, Company E.
Daniel Harwell, Company E.
Josh Burnett, Company B.
Miles Mewborn, Company B.
Rufus Purdy, Company I.
Daniel Jones, Company L.
Ben Parham, Company L.
Royal Winston, Company G.
Frank Chrisman, Company G.
Mat Elam, Company C.

In at least two instances proof was given by the slave of heroic devotion to his master. Lieutenant Thurman was shot at Atlanta, and his body servant, Young, taking charge of him, through all sorts of hardships and deprivations, faithfully nursed him until he died. Young then dug a grave with his own hands, buried his young master, and, making his way across two States, came back to Shelby county, where the stricken father and mother heard the pitiful story from his lips of how their boy had passed away. They told Young that they wanted their boy buried at their old home; so the negro, with a wagon and team, made his way back to the unmarked grave he had dug and brought the body all the way through a thousand difficulties and dangers to the old master and mistress. I do not know that this negro is now living, but I mention his deed that those of this generation may know something of a faithfulness strong enough and great enough to command the admiration of all the world.

Another: At Belmont one of the negroes, whose name I deeply regret having lost, while the battle was yet raging, seeing his young master fall, went into the storm of shot and shell and brought the body safely back into our lines. In Edwards' beautiful story of "The Valley of the Shadder" a similar episode is told—so eloquently, so tenderly told—that it is difficult to read it without tears. The Thirteenth Regiment saw the actual occurrence at Belmont, so can bear witness for the negro to those who might think Mr. Edwards was speaking from his fancy rather than from actual facts.

Now my task is done. If this humble compilation will save from obscurity some of my old comrades—if it will add anything to the record of the fame which others have won—I have received all the reward I ask.

APPENDIX.

Some Incidents of the War.

Some incidents and happenings took place during the war which, I think, would interest or amuse, and which do not strictly form a part of this brief compilation. I add some of them here in the hope that they may not be found dull reading to those who have followed thus far my little contribution.

A FLAG PRESENTATION.

This incident occurred just as the Dixie Rifles were on the eve of leaving home to go into the army, and was swallowed up in the vortex of the terrible war we then thought was to be of such short duration. I think to mention it now, for its blending of the beautiful and ludicrous will bring it back to the minds of the survivors and their descendants of Company E of the old Thirteenth Regiment.

On a glorious June morning, with just that buoyancy in the air that makes mere existence a pleasure, the company assembled in the little village of Moscow, Fayette county, to receive a most beautiful and elegant Confederate flag that the ladies of the village had made for the company. The then Miss Fannie Steger (now Mrs. Dr. R. L. Knox of Memphis) had been selected to make the presentation of the colors. I do not know if she will thank me now for attempting to bring back the speech that she, a winsome and lovely young lady, made to us on that morning. Of course I cannot recall all that she said, but I can remember enough to know that it sounded like the blast of a bugle, like the playing of exquisite music, and inspired every member of the company with intenser patriotism and with profound admiration for the fair speaker. Feeling myself (then as now) utterly incapable of making a speech, I called on a young member of the company to receive the flag from the fair hands of those who had woven it. He stepped on the platform with every appearance of self-confidence, but to his surprise and to that of all the rest of us, he found himself overwhelmed with embarrassment. Blushing, stuttering and stammering, he began with, "Ladies and gentlemen, we accept," and then broke down. After swallowing a glass or two of water, he began again, "Ladies and gentlemen, we accept," and, still stammering and stuttering, once more took water. This occurred a third time, when one of the boys called out from the rear, "D—n it, say to her, We accept the flag, and will follow it to h
—l or to victory." Amid yells of applause the young man reached for the flag

and sat down. This flag was kept throughout the whole war, and today, thirty-two years since the struggle ended, is carefully preserved by my friend, Dr. T. B. Yancey, of Somerville, Tenn.

THE PRESENTATION OF A HORSE.

While the army was in winter quarters at Dalton, Ga., an incident occurred in the Thirteenth Tennessee Regiment which has left a memory that will linger with me until the "shadows gather for the eternal night."

The regiment was reduced to less than two hundred men, and, in generosity and love, these few men determined to make me (now promoted to Brigadier-General) a present of a horse. It was difficult to find such a horse as they wanted, but Dr. Yandell of Louisville, Ky., who belonged to the medical department, had a magnificent Gray Eagle horse, for which he wanted four thousand dollars, but said that, if the regiment wanted it for their commander, he would take three thousand dollars. These few men, drawing eleven dollars per month, with their uniforms in rags, and living on half rations, agreed to buy the horse, and absolutely refused to let anyone outside of the regiment give one cent. The money was scraped up among themselves and the present made, Captain Jerry Crook of Company I delivering the presentation speech, and Captain R. F. Lanier of Company G, on behalf of his commander, the reception speech. The horse was christened "Chickamauga." I have lived to forget many things, but never will pass from my heart the gratitude I felt that day when my war-worn soldiers in their ragged gray gathered around me to show their love and confidence. If nothing else, that act alone makes dear to my heart every soldier of the Thirteenth Tennessee Regiment.

MY LOST LEG.

Among the most intimate friends of my evening time, I have found infinite comfort and cheer in two, who for twenty years have been a part of my life. These two, the Hon. James M. Greer and Mr. James F. Hunter, having made me almost a part of their family lives, I wrote out for their boys, Allen, Autry and Rowan Greer, and Douglass Hunter, this account of how I lost my leg, and print it here without apology to my readers.

Soon after Sherman's army was so signally repulsed on the Kennesaw line, he again commenced his flank movement, which forced our army to fall back.

On the 4th of July, 1864, one of the hottest days of the season, our army arrived at Vining Station, just below Marietta, Ga., where it was formed in line of battle, with orders for each brigade to intrench and throw up breastworks.

I was busily engaged all the morning in superintending the work, which was about completed between 12 and 1 o'clock, when, with my staff, I retired to a large spreading oak tree, about 150 or 200 yards in the rear of my line of works, to rest and to eat my scanty rations. No fighting was going on at this time except an artillery duel between a Federal battery some distance off and a Confederate battery on my line.

After I had eaten up all the rations I had, I concluded I would take a smoke. Matches in those days were very scarce and hard to get; so I always carried with me a small sunglass to light my pipe with when the sun was shining. After tilling my pipe I noticed that the sun was shining through a small opening in the foliage of the tree under which I was sitting, and I remarked to Colonel Dyer, my Inspector-General, that I could light my pipe through the little opening. He replied that he would bet me a drink of pine-top whisky that I could not. I accepted the bet (as I was then not as punctilious about betting as I am now), and just as I was in the act of drawing a focus on my tobacco, a shell from the enemy's battery came whizzing through the air over my line and exploded just as it struck my foot and the ground, tearing off my foot and making a hole almost large enough to bury me in.

My staff were lying around under the shade of the tree, but none of them were struck by the shell or any of its fragments. Col. Dyer, who was standing over me at the time, had nearly all his clothing torn off, not by the shell or its fragments, but by the gravel that was thrown up against him. He received seventeen flesh wounds, none of which proved very serious. As soon as the shell exploded he involuntarily started to run to get behind a tree. A few days before this Col. Dyer and myself, while walking in the rear of our line on Kennesaw Mountain, noticed that a soldier with all the canteens of his company swung around him, was going after water for his company, when a schrapnel shell came over, exploded and riddled him with balls; yet he walked, or rather ran, some little distance before falling, and then fell dead. Col. Dyer told me that he had this man in his mind's eye while running, and he expected every moment to fall dead.

The shock from the explosion of the shell was very severe, yet the tearing away of my leg was accompanied by neither pain nor the loss of much blood. In addition to the loss of my foot I received another wound on my other leg which was rather remarkable. I had a cut below the knee about four inches long and down to the bone, as smooth as if it had been cut with a sharp knife, yet neither my pants nor underclothing were torn. It was so smooth a cut that when pressed together it healed by first intention. None of us were able to conjecture what made this cut. Before I would allow my removal I made my staff find my sunglass and my pipe. The rim of my sunglass was broken.

As soon as it was known that I was wounded, the surgeons of my brigade and division came to my assistance, and bound up my wounds as best they could, and gave me some morphine and whisky. I was then put in an ambulance and started to the field hospital. In going to the hospital I passed by Gen. Cheatham's headquarters, who, hearing that I was wounded, came out to sympathize with me, and suggested that as I was looking very pale he thought that some stimulant would do me good, and gave me a stiff drink. I then began to feel pretty good and proceeded on my way to the hospital. I had not gone very far when I passed Gen. Hardee's headquarters. He had heard of my misfortune and came out to see me. He also said I was looking very pale and that I ought to have some stimulant, and gave me a big drink. I continued to feel better, and again started toward the hospital, and in a short time passed Gen. Joseph E. Johnston's headquarters. He came out to see me and also said that I was looking very pale, and that some stimulant would do me good. He happened to have some very fine apple brandy, and gave me a big drink, and down it went. From this time on I knew nothing until I awoke on the platform at Atlanta at sunrise next morning.

The amputation of my leg at the point selected was an unfortunate one for me. My brigade surgeon, Dr. R. W. Mitchell, was absent at the time of my arrival at the field hospital, and the point of selection for the amputation was determined upon by a consultation of surgeons before he returned. If my leg had been cut off higher up it would have relieved me of the many days of suffering I have since experienced.

From Atlanta I was carried on a freight train in a box car, in the hottest of weather, to Macon, Ga. Dr. Mitchell accompanied me, thinking I would die before I reached the place. My sufferings were intense, but I survived, and was taken to Mrs. Josie, the wife of a quartermaster of my division of the army, who cared for and treated me as kindly as if I had been her own child.

Thus I lost my leg, and I have never seen it since.

The Famous Snowball Battle

IN THE CONFEDERATE ARMY AT DALTON, GA., 1864.

BY GENERAL GEO. W. GORDON.
(By request.)

That subdivision of the Confederate forces, known as the "Army of Tennessee," and then commanded by General Jos. E. Johnston, passed the memorable winter of 1863-4 in camp at Dalton, Ga. The winter was one of unprecedented severity—the thermometer registering in January, 1864, three degrees below zero. During the cold weather an unusual amount of snow fell for that latitude; and the chief occupations of the soldiers were getting wood, cooking, eating, and keeping warm. It was too cold to drill or to indulge in the usual out-door games, "stag dances," etc., tents being too small for these purposes. And as most of the "boys" were *young* men, naturally there was an accumulation of physical energy that constantly sought issue in athletic exercises. When the copious fall of snow came, it brought the opportunity not only for exercise, but for royal sport as well. But before proceeding further, let us explain that in selecting a camp, the subdivisions of the same command are placed as near together as sanitation, water supplies, the conformation of the ground and general convenience, will allow. That is to say, the regiments of a brigade are located near each other. So, the brigades of a division; and so the divisions of an army corps. General B. F. Cheatham's Division of General Hardee's Corps, was composed of four brigades of Tennesseeans,—Maney's, Vaughan's, Carter's and Strahl's, and was camped on one side of a considerable depression in the ground, not sharp enough to be called a ravine, but through which a small branch ran during wet weather. On the opposite summit and slope to this depression, and about three hundred paces from the Tennesseeans, was camped Gen. Walker's Division of Georgia troops—also of Gen. Hardee's Corps.

The day after the snow had ceased to fall, "snow-balling" first began among the men of the same companies and camps, and many interesting, exciting and clamorous contests were had for several hours. But finally a body of Tennesseeans and Georgians became arrayed against each other and very soon the contest became highly exciting. As the news spread through the camps that a fight was on hand between the Georgians and Tennesseeans, division pride and State pride became excited, the small fights ceased, and reinforcements poured in to both sides of the State forces until all interest was absorbed in one grand battle between Georgians and Tennesseeans, in which several thousand men were now engaged, making the heavens wild with shouts and the air striped with the tracks of flying snow-balls. Charge after charge was made and repulsed. Shout after shout rent the sky. For two hours or longer the battle raged, with partially varying successes. The prisoners who were captured in one charge would make their escape under the excitement of the next, and rejoin their comrades in the fight. Sometimes the assaulting columns would have to retreat because their ammunition would give out, and would, in turn, be countercharged and routed by the receiving forces who had held their ground and defended their magazines (large piles of snow-balls as high as a man's head all along the line and prepared beforehand) and were thus supplied with ammunition. Sometimes these magazines would be charged and captured by massing a force for that purpose. In these charges the supreme efforts made by the defending forces to resist the momentum of the assaulting mass, raised excitement to its wildest height. The place where a magazine was captured was always retaken, but sometimes not until the ammunition had been used up on those making it, or carried away by the enemy into his own lines. Finally, after alternating successes of a very partial and indecisive character, the battle ceased as if by common consent and the weary combatants "rested upon their arms"—each upon his original ground and upon opposite sides of the depression, or small branch before referred to, and not more than a hundred paces apart. Neither side seemed to be satisfied. Neither was whipped and neither appeared inclined to leave the field. Besides, during this cessation of hostilities, both armies were vigorously engaged in making ammunition, which, with other demonstrations of a hostile character, clearly indicated that the battle was soon to be renewed and upon a much grander and more imposing scale than ever before.

Up to this juncture, the writer had been only a highly interested spectator of the contest from a distance, and had not expected to take any personal part in the fight. But at this moment, a messenger, and one of my own command, came running to my quarters and said that he had been sent by the Tennesseeans to ask me to come and command them, and to come mounted; that with a mounted commander to lead them, they thought they could win the fight. With my interest already highly excited, it needed no persuasion, and I told my colored boy to saddle my horse immediately. By the time he had done so, the messenger had improvised a flag for me to carry, out of an old bandanna handkerchief, about two feet and a half square, and the largest and dirtiest one, I think, I ever saw. I mounted my horse, a beautiful dappled iron grey, and with the bandanna flag in my hand, flying to the breeze, I charged to the field—my horse leaping logs, ditches and other obstructions and running faster as I approached the exciting scene. When I checked up in front of the Tennesseeans, (now in battle array) and waving my flag, such a tremendous shout shook the air that the very atmosphere seemed to quiver around and above us. Excitement was now intense, and the men wildly impatient to make the charge. Immediately after my appearance on horse-back in front of the Tennesseeans, Major ——, (whose name I regret to have forgotten) of Gen. Walker's staff, appeared mounted at the head of the Georgians. His coming was greeted with a tremendous shout from *his* men, and was answered by mine with another shout, as if to say: "We accept your challenge." Excitement was now extreme. Non-combatants had assembled by hundreds on the surrounding hills and house-tops to see the fight. General officers and their staffs, at their headquarters, had mounted their horses or ascended higher elevations to witness the impending struggle. All was now ready. And after directing the men to fill their pockets, bosoms and hands with balls, and the ordnance officers to follow the line with all the ammunition their details could carry, I ordered the charge. With a shout that signaled victory, and an impetuosity that seemed irresistible, we dashed upon the brave Georgians, and for a few minutes the struggle was fierce and furious, desperate and doubtful. The air was white with whizzing and bursting balls; men were tripped up, knocked down, covered with snow, or run over. The writer was struck with at least a hundred balls, and his horse by as many more. The momentum of the charging column was too great, however, to be successfully resisted, more especially so when it outflanked both wings of the enemy, which soon gave way. The center then being flanked, and at the same time being sorely pressed in front, also gave way, and his entire army fled in great confusion. The rout on the field was now complete, and the enemy was not only driven therefrom, but through his own camp and into the woods beyond. The object of the campaign (victory) being now accomplished, I ordered the pursuit to cease and the men to return to their camps. As they did so, however, some of them stopped in the deserted camps of the Georgians and plundered their mess chests, which had been well filled by supplies from their friends at home. When I heard of this, and reproved it as not being a legitimate object of the campaign, the reply and defense were in that questionable old maxim, "All is fair in love and war."

So far from this episode of camp life having been a source of unkind feeling between Walker's Division of Georgians and Cheatham's Division of Tennesseeans, it ever afterward seemed to be rather a bond of sympathy and union. The writer never afterward passed or met the Georgia Division, that its men did not greet him with shouts, often with "Three cheers for the Snowball Colonel!" "Colonel" was my rank at the time and "The Snowball Colonel" was the designation they ever afterward gave me. This "snowball battle" seems to have made a deep and indelible impression on all the soldiers who took part in, or who witnessed it; for one of the first questions I am often asked by old soldiers whom I have not seen since the close of the war, is: "General, do you remember the snowball battle at Dalton, Ga.?" This, and the additional fact that it is still so often a topic of conversation among the old soldiers, is, I suppose, why Gen. Vaughan has requested me to write an account of it as an appendix to his book.

In concluding this report of the celebrated snowball fight, I suppose the writer can say, without being charged with vanity, that he won more "reputation" ("that idle and most false imposition; often got without merit and lost without deserving") than in all the other battles in which he participated during the war. He is said to have performed prodigies of daring and desperation during the action, as men can generally do when there is not much danger in front, and no disgrace in defeat. With a bowed head (after the manner of a pugnacious sheep) to protect his face and eyes from the balls of the enemy, he rode right into and through their ranks, amid a deluging snowstorm of flying missiles, and emerged therefrom with a floating flag, but a hatless head. He congratulates his command and himself that though the battle was intensely boisterous, it was practically bloodless—the only casualties being a few blinded eyes and two or three broken arms, during an action in which not fewer than five thousand men were engaged.

The Tennesseeans were so enthused with their great victory over the Georgians, that they wanted another fight before the "weary sun," then sinking low, "had made his golden set." But as there was not time to seek it with troops in a distant camp and from a different State, they concluded to fight each other. Accordingly an issue was joined between Maney's Brigade, commanded by Col. Hume Field, mounted, and Vaughan's Brigade, commanded by the writer, also mounted. The dispositions for battle having been duly made, the charge was mutually sounded, and when the opposing lines, advancing on each other with great speed and impetuosity, clashed, the shock was tremendous. Men fell right and left, in front and rear. Some were dragged from the field, hatless and coatless, amid the greatest cheering and wildest shouts. "When Greek meets Greek, then comes the *tug* of war." The battle raged till all the reserves had been brought into action, when a supreme effort was made by both sides to close the fight with victory. The writer, venturing too far into the enemy's ranks, had his horse seized by as many of them as could get hold of him, and was thrown to the ground; the rider was grabbed by the head and arms (his bandanna flag going down in the wreck), and was being dragged to the enemy's rear, when a large squad of his own men seized him by the other end in an effort to recapture him, and he was raised from the ground and actually strung up between the heavens and the earth by the pulling forces at each end of him. At this moment he *felt* that his situation was now serious indeed, and that it was time to stop such "d—n foolishness." So, by vigorous kicking, "cussing" and yelling to his men to release him, they did so, and he was left a prisoner in the hands of the enemy, but without any serious injury. In the meantime, however, his own men had captured the commander of the enemy, and as neither side now had a leader the men ceased fighting and entered into negotiations for an exchange of prisoners. By the time the exchange was effected, the ardor of the combatants had greatly cooled, and neither side seemed disposed to renew the contest.

As to the result of the fight, it may be called a drawn battle, or described by an anecdote of a darkey attached as a servant to Gen. Floyd's command in Virginia. When Gen. Floyd had been beaten and was being pursued by the enemy, the darkey moved to the rear far in advance of the retreating troops, and when he was met by a soldier going to join the command and was asked what was the news from Gen. Floyd, he did not want to admit that he had been defeated, but said: "When I lef 'em, our men wuz vancin backwards on de Yankees, and dey wuz retreatin on us." As the last beams of the setting sun gilded the icy branches of the leafless trees with the beauteous tints of the rainbow, the soldiers returned to their camps from the white field of the great "snowball battle," and retired that night with the fadeless memory of a glorious day.

www.ingramcontent.com/pod-product-compliance
Lightning Source LLC
Chambersburg PA
CBHW060801310726
48980CB00002B/181

9783732623327